Caution:

Reading this book by lonely women may result in extreme stimulation, lust and exquisite languor.

Brought to you by
Indigo After Dark
an Imprint of
Genesis Press, Inc.

Indigo After Dark

is published by

Genesis Press, Inc.

315 Third Avenue North
Columbus, MS 39701

Copyright© 2000 by Vicki Andrews and Donna Hill

Indigo After Dark Vol. I
Midnight Erotic Fantasies & In Between the Night

ISBN: 0-7394-1728-2

Manufactured in the United States of America

First Edition

Indigo After Dark

Vol. I

Romantic Erotica ... for women

Genesis Press, Inc.

Indigo After Dark

Genesis Press's new imprint goes beyond sensuous. It's romantic erotica that is tasteful, classy and vividly sexual—in short, it's hot but not pornographic. Here's what some of the readers had to say about Indigo After Dark.

The stories give just the amount of tease to entice the reader to breathe hard and wish to be inside the pages of the book. Thank you, Tracye.

I'm in my twelfth year of marriage, and reading these stories gives me plenty of ideas and helps me to recreate the romance that has dwindled away.

MORE, MORE, MORE! This is exactly what I've been waiting for—AA romance. Bravo Genesis!.

This is great!! It's erotic without being vulgar. I can't wait until this line is on the book shelves.

Romantic, yes, but even more so, in a sexy romantic type of fantasy. These stories seem to be geared toward a more mature female reader, like myself.

I think this is just what we need, some seduction along with some romance. I'll definitely buy this book.

The sexual overtures were a turn on. It's nice to know that passion exists between two people. Can't wait for the book to come out.

So go on, what are you waiting for? Your fantasies await you on the other side of this page. Indulge.

Indigo After Dark...
Beyond Sensuous

Vol. I

Midnight Erotic Fantasies
By
Nia Dixon

In Between the Night
By
Angelique

Table of Contents

Midnight Erotic Fantasies
By
Nia Dixon

Midnight Erotic

Fantasies

by

Nia Dixon

Body Doc

*A*s requests go, this had to be the most unusual one yet. You see I'm a writer, a writer searching for a phenomenal artist to produce the most dramatic, sensual, and provocative cover I've ever had. People respond to visual stimuli and, of course, sex sells. I needed something so provocative that the picture would leap off the cover into the readers' hands, while my story inside would touch their hearts. That's what I needed.

In my search, one of my dear friends, Darlene, said she'd heard about an artist whose work "sang" off the canvas. She said they call him Body Doc. His name alone was enough to entice me to contact him. Some artists are arrogant, I know that, but this man would not bring his work to me; I had to go to him, to his home, which was also his studio. When he asked me to meet him there, I wanted to refuse, but since Darlene recommended him and said he was one of the best, I acquiesced, scribbled down directions to his home, and hoped his art was as good as I wanted it to be.

When I arrived, the building's architectural design was unusual, somewhat gothic and dark, but the higher floors had lots of windows. I couldn't imagine working, much less living there. But that wasn't my business, now was it? I reminded myself. I knocked on the massive solid wood door, bruising my knuckles. I hadn't expected the wood to be so unyieldy. I was shaking my hand and kissing my knuckles when he answered the door. He was—to use a cliché—tall, dark, and handsome. This brotha had it going on. He was fine, and I do mean fine. I guess I stood there a tad too long just looking at him. Then he smiled, and I finally found my voice.

"Are you Body Doc?" I inquired timidly.

"That would be me. Come in." He pushed the heavy door open, stepped aside so I could enter.

His loft smelled of paint. Acrylics and oil paintings sprinkled every inch of the walls; canvases dotted the floor. The room was massive, with one wall of floor-to-ceiling windows. I noticed an enormous drafting board that dominated one corner, and I could see he was working on a drawing of a partially nude black woman. She had enormous breasts and beautiful gray eyes that held a level of intrigue and mystery that was captivating. Her lips were slightly parted as if she were breathless, and her hair was tousled as if she'd just been screwed. There was a hint of animalistic hunger in her eyes—in her posture a certain flicker of desire—her back was arched and the strap of her dress had fallen, dangling suggestively off her shoulder, revealing a breast.

"Nice work," I said, gesturing to the drawing.

"Thanks."

"Live model?" I questioned.

"Not really," he coyly replied. "She's only alive inside my head."

I gazed at the sketch again and was amazed that in his head would be such detail—fine lines around her mouth, a mole on her cheek, visible veins on her chest. His detail was inclusive, right down to the dark areola and tiny raised bumps around her nipples.

I could feel him looking at me. His eyes seemed to bore a hole in my back. I turned to see that he was staring at my legs, openly surveying them up and down—slowly, deliberately. I cleared my throat, turning my full attention to him, and asked to see more of his work. My voice had a slight tremble, and that unnerved me.

While he went to retrieve drawings he thought were suitable—he already knew what I was looking for—I took a moment to survey the room again. His loft left much to be desired in terms of furnishings. What little he had was covered by various materials. When he returned carrying a large portfolio, we were forced to sit on the floor. I sat crossing my legs at the ankle, mindful that I had on a skirt. I flipped through his portfolio, very aware of his presence so near to me. He lazily lay back, propping himself up on one elbow. He wore a T-shirt, baggy shorts, and no shoes. I glanced at him, and he was smiling at me in a knowing sort of way. I quickly averted my gaze from his smiling lips to the drawings laid before me. I was unable to concentrate. I felt as if he were lurking nearer to me, closer and closer, but when I looked at him again, he hadn't moved, but that same expression remained on his face.

"These are beautiful," I exclaimed, somewhat breathlessly, closing the portfolio.

"As are you," he replied.

I became flustered, heat raced up my face, no doubt flushing it. While most darker-skinned black people don't blush, I have the audacity to be one who does. I was instantly embarrassed. I lowered my head again and opened the portfolio to look at what I'd already seen. My mind flew in different directions, I didn't really see the paintings because suddenly I was aware of so many other things: The sexy tones of Maxwell singing "Sumthin', Sumthin' " on the *Love Jones* soundtrack played softly nearby, and the scents of the room became overwhelming; they seemed to swirl about my head. I felt dizzy—dizzy with desire—a feeling that I thought had escaped me long ago. But I knew it when it came, and it surprised me that it came now.

He shifted slightly, and to my complete and utter surprise I could see the head of his penis peeking innocently out from his baggy shorts. I gasped. It was a beautiful penis, obviously very long, the head smooth. I felt heat rise between my legs, and I wanted to tell him that he was inadvertently exposing himself. But when I looked into his eyes, I had a feeling he already knew.

For reasons I could not understand, I wanted to kiss him—hard—for a very long time. I wanted to get lost inside the essence of him, his smile, his creative mind, his spirit. It was all so weird, this feeling that had crept over me.

As I returned my attention to his drawings yet again—I had to really for I was getting lost inside an emotion that was somewhat foreign to me. Certainly upon first meeting a man, I never felt this sexual, this alive with sensuality, but he somehow did this to me. And when he spoke, his voice sounded so much like a melody, he could have been singing. He crooned words that were somewhat poetic and sensuous.

"I want to taste you," he said matter-of-factly in a hoarse whisper.

Startled, I gazed upon him, and a sexy smile held his face captive. Then, he rose to his knees and inched so close to me that I could smell traces of his last cigarette, which lingered on his breath, the fragrance of his cologne tinged the air around me and left a metallic taste in my mouth. My panties became moist with desire and readiness. I did not recoil or move away from him. I wanted this kiss. And I wanted to taste him, too.

His kiss was tender and slow, a toying of lips upon lips, a gentle battle between tongues. His hand timidly grazed one breast, then he cupped it, as if feeling for its size and measuring its weight. He rolled my nipple between thumb and finger causing it to rise. My head began to swim, and I trembled at his touch. With ease he laid me down, settling comfortably between my thighs. I should have been embarrassed at the wetness of my panties, but I was not, for desire was sweeping me away, and I wanted nothing more than to feel his generous penis deep inside me, filling my walls, touching my womb.

His hips, much slimmer than mine, began to rock, to teeter precariously above me, then plunge and rock some more. I could feel the heat as it began to rise between my raised skirt and his loose shorts. He kept up this rhythm of toying with me until I could stand no more. I clawed at the elastic around his waist, pulling his shorts down in one fell swoop. His penis was hard and rigid, standing at attention, waiting to service me. I held it in my hands and stroked his shaft. I kissed the tip timidly at first, inhaling his scent and loving it. I teased him with quick, wet strokes, but did not take all of him into my mouth. For now, I was content to suckle his head. My mouth formed a rather large O once I did begin to swallow him whole, inch by glorious inch, until his penis touched the back of my throat. I sucked him, tasting the sweet nectar he left upon my tongue. I held his balls in my hand, cradled them as gently as I could, then I stroked them with my tongue, kissing each one tenderly. I felt him tremble, then heard him cry out, "Oh, God."

Yes, I thought, oh, yes.

He withdrew himself from my mouth and helped me wiggle out of my now very soaked panties. He held them in his hand, then sniffed them, inhaling deeply my sex scent. I watched him in amazement. He tossed them aside. Roughly, he used his knees to nudge my legs apart. I could feel myself oozing love juices back to my rectum—I'm sure a pool was forming behind me. For a time, he just looked at me as though mesmerized. I wondered how I looked to him all pink and swollen and oozing. Like a snake, his hot tongue quickly grazed my clit, which was hard and standing at attention. He licked it again and again and again, quickly, not lingering, like being engaged in a jab-then-run fight. I wanted more. I clamped my thighs around his ears and held him there. He understood. His mouth covered my entire vagina, and his tongue stroked me mercilessly, gaining a rhythm that matched the rocking of my hips. His tongue darted in and out of me, gave my clit a serious workout, and I began to shake. A trembling started deep in my belly, a cold sweat covered my body, as more sweat dripped from the backs of my knees. I felt my nipples harden. I was in heaven. My breath was ragged and harsh, coming faster and faster. I was about to cum.

The first rise of the contraction started low. I felt a tingling sen-sation that started with my toes, then the feeling engulfed my entire body like a small shower of sparks had begun to invade me in the most delicate of places. A powerful parade of contractions pulsed through my vagina, spraying juices everywhere. My clit bounced and jumped, and he couldn't keep hold of it. I literally cried out, sounding like a bear growling. I throbbed rhythmically for at least a dozen beats, and I thought I'd lose my mind with the pleasure coursing through me. He lapped up all my juices then inserted a finger into my anus. I gasped, shocked at this invasion, until I felt that familiar tingling begin again. This was heaven. His touch was gentle, the probing invasive but not unpleasant. I felt my body responding again as more juices trickled from me to rest in his palm.

Finally, he entered me. I tensed my muscles around him, pulling him in as he pushed. He withdrew, then did it again. It seemed he got longer and longer with each new insertion, and I wanted him to continue to grow until his penis was touching the back of my throat. He filled me up, and I felt my walls hungrily accepting him, wanting more. I bucked wildly at each new penetration. I felt as if I were losing my mind, losing myself, with each stroke. I opened my eyes and found him staring at me, a satisfied smirk upon his face. Now I knew how he could be so detailed in his paintings of women. For I was sure if I looked in a mirror I would see in my eyes the very same intense gaze as I had seen on the sketch of the woman earlier.

Then, he came in a great spasmodic rush, and I could feel each pump of semen from his body into mine. My vaginal walls squeezed then released him, sucking his liquid like a tongue lapping up the last bit of gravy.

For a time, we lay side by side languishing in pleasure, too weak to speak. And really, no words were necessary. Our bodies had said it all. Eventually my pulse slowed, and my breathing returned to normal.

I rolled over and asked, "Is this why they call you Body Doc?"

A knowing smile crept over his lips, he nodded, then said, "Yes, and by the way, I do make house calls."

"You do?" I coyly responded.

"Yes," he said and raised himself up to look into my eyes. "And I'd very much like to see you again."

"Really," I paused. "Why?" I had to know. I had to ask.

"There's a power inside you I want to get to know."

"Power? What kind of power?"

"It's indescribable really. It's just a feeling I got about you."

"Do you make love to every woman who comes here?"

"No."

Did I believe him? Not really. Suddenly this whole thing seemed so crazy, so unreal. I laughed aloud, then I grew very serious, "So...when do you plan to sketch me?"

The Handyman

A
s a new home owner, Tanya Moore was ecstatic as she entered the so-called realm of being a buppy—a single, black professional female. Everything Tanya wanted was coming to fruition and now with the purchase of her first home, albeit a fixer-upper, but nonetheless her home, life was falling into order the way she wanted it to. When Tanya first bought the house, she thought it was such a fantastic bargain. All it needed, she reasoned, was a little love, some weed pulling, a coat of paint or two, and it would be good as new. That was before she actually moved in and found her bargain house needed lots and lots of repairs—things she was unable to do herself kept creeping up. To make matters worse, she was truly limited in fix-it skills, but that didn't stop her. She wanted this house—could afford this house—and she would do whatever it took to make it beautiful.

Tanya realized she was in serious need of help when she walked down the stairs one day, and the railing fell off, nearly crushing her toes as she fell back and screeched. She cursed at herself and the railing, then proceeded to put it back on. Upon further examination, she realized the holes in which the screws fit were stripped, and no matter how many times she tried, the rail just wouldn't hold. What do you do when this happens? she wondered. Then later, when she went to turn the light on in her walk-in closet, it snapped, the light diminishing quickly, like a flash of lightning. She peered at the fixture for some time before finally retreating to the garage to retrieve her newly purchased ladder. She tried to pull off the globe but it wouldn't budge. She struggled with it until sweat ran down her arms and into her eyes. All to no avail. If she couldn't see her clothes and boxes of shoes, how would she get her wardrobe coordinated in the morning? Something had to be done, and it had to be done soon. She had other single friends, what did they do? She called Sherri first.

"Hey, girl, what's going on," Sherri cheerfully said once she knew it was Tanya calling.

"My house is falling apart around my ears."

She heard Sherri gasp. "W-h-a-t?"

"It's mostly minor repairs, but I don't know how to do this stuff. I need some help. You know anybody?"

"No, girl, my brother does stuff for me when I can catch him."

"Do you think he'd help me out, too?" Tanya asked, distressed.

"I don't know, girl. He's hard to catch up with. It takes him forever to come help me."

"I gotta do something. Okay, let me look in the yellow pages."

"The yellow pages!" Sherri screeched. "Girl, you don't know who you gonna get if you do that. You don't want just anybody up in your house."

"Aren't they licensed or something?"

"Licensed? Who cares about a license? The question is are you going to be safe once this person has had access to your home. I wouldn't do it if I were you," Sherri admonished.

Tanya sighed. "You're probably right. This is when having a man comes in handy—seriously," she said, smirking.

"Not to mention those cold, lonely nights, huh?"

"Now you know you didn't even have to go there." She chuckled. "I'll figure something out. I'll talk to you later."

Tanya sat in quiet contemplation for some time, agonizing about her problems. She climbed the ladder again, fought with the light fixture till large sweat rings appeared on her shirt; then sweat trickled slowly down the middle of her back. Finally conceding defeat, she ran an extension cord into the closet and propped a lamp on boxes of shoes on the closet floor.

"There," she said to herself. "That'll have to do for now."

Anxious to fill her cabinets with food, Tanya went to the grocery store at nine o'clock. The hour was late, she knew that, but she also thought that at this time of night she wouldn't have to wait in a long line or watch where she was going—no worries about colliding with another shopper's cart, or listening to screeching, demanding children whine as parents cajoled and tolerated tantrums.

Up and down the aisles she went, surveying, pricing, and picking all kinds of items for her new house. She needed absolutely everything it seemed: wax for the wood floors, glass cleaner for outside windows, ant and bug repellent (she thought she saw some critters), and a plethora of other things. She wasn't tired so she took her time, muttered to herself when something was outrageously priced, did a little jig when she found a bargain, was actually having fun shopping for the first time in her life.

Troy shopped at night simply because he never had time to do it during the day. As a handyman he rushed from one house to the next fixing, repairing, hammering, and consoling those who were clueless—some for real, some faking—so he couldn't do his own shopping when other people did. He had a scowl on his face until he saw Tanya's round ass jiggling in Aisle Ten. He watched her for a time. She was funny. She would mutter to herself, scratch her head, pick up, put back, then she'd do a little dance once she finally decided on something. He laughed aloud.

Tanya stopped, quickly turning to the sound of the laughter, hoping against hope that someone hadn't seen her acting like a fool. She saw a very tall, muscular brother standing there smiling at her, his smile lopsided, his coveralls and boots dirty and caked with mud.

Damn that, he was gorgeous!

"Looks like you're having fun," he said.

Tanya was embarrassed. "A little too much fun," she finally answered.

"Ain't nothing wrong with that. I guess if you've got to do it, especially this late, you might as well have fun."

"I just bought my first house, and I guess that's what's making me giddy."

"Ahhh," he said. "Just signed your life away, huh?"

She laughed. "Yeah, it did feel like that. So many loan documents and so much money. It was scary."

"But the best thing you've ever done, am I right?"

"Yes," she said and smiled at him again.

"My name's Troy," he said, extending his powerful hand for her to grip.

"Tanya."

"We're probably neighbors. I live on Scranton Court."

"I'm not totally familiar with all the streets yet, but I'm on Sparrow Way."

"Two streets over, north," he advised.

"Oh," she said, shaking her head, watching him, trying to check out his ring finger.

"I'm surprised your husband isn't with you. It's almost ten," he said while avoiding her gaze to glance at his watch.

"No husband," she replied. "Wife?"

"Nope," he answered. Then: "Boyfriend?" he inquired, raising one bushy eyebrow.

"Ditto—no boyfriend. . .girlfriend?"

"Not anymore," came his reply, coupled with an easy smile. "Did I introduce myself?"

"Yes," she said, laughing. "You did."

"I must seem really nosy to you, huh?"

"More like curious, I'd say. After all, I am a new face to the neighborhood."

"A new black face," he clarified.

11

"Okay," she conceded.

"And what a pretty face it is."

She felt the heated blush rise to her cheeks. "Thank you."

"May I make another bold statement...and observation?" he asked.

"Why stop now," she teased.

"That little screwdriver set you've got there," he said, pointing to her bargain $2.99 assorted screwdriver set.

"Yeah."

"It ain't gonna work. Too flimsy."

"Not to mention cheap," she chimed in, plucking it from the cart.

"Yeah, that too."

"What do you recommend? I'm starting to notice small repairs that need to be done, and I don't know how to fix them or what tools I really need."

"It must be fate that brought us together tonight to meet in Safeway."

"You think," she replied. "Why is that?"

"I'm a handyman. Fix all kind of problems for people. That's how I make my living."

"Ohhh," she crooned. "I see. I need a handyman."

"Music to my ears," he said and smiled.

"Are you expensive?"

"That depends on what you want me to do. What do you need, Tanya?"

She studied his face for a while, wondered *Is he flirting with me.* "I need lots of things," she answered, flinging a sexy, sassy retort at him.

"Can you be a bit more specific?"

She made a decision very quickly, tossed the screwdriver set back into her cart, scribbled her address and telephone number on the shopping list she held in her hand and handed it to him. "Here. Call me. Let's talk."

He studied her handwriting, a beautifully sculpted script. "Okay. I'll give you a call."

She grabbed the handle of her cart and said over her shoulder, "Soon, okay?" And with her heart pounding hard, she turned the corner and gave herself permission to breathe.

He is handsome, articulate, single, and a handyman. And darned if he wasn't flirting with me. It doesn't get any better than this, she thought.

Once she had finally finished her shopping, she couldn't help but look around for him, hoping he was still there somewhere. Initially she casually glanced around but when she still hadn't spotted him, she began turning her head left and right, almost frantically waiting and wanting him to appear. But she didn't see him. Finally she conceded that he was probably gone. She wanted to kick herself. She now realized that in her haste to be coy, she had given him her number but didn't get his. That might have been a mistake.

ॐ

Early Saturday morning Tanya was busy lining her kitchen cabinets with colorful Contact paper. She faintly heard the doorbell chime over the music she was blasting. Her hair was tied back under an old, colorful silk scarf, her face was devoid of makeup, she had thrown on old sweats, had even rolled up the sleeves since she was ready to work. She turned down the music as she passed the stereo, answered the door with a breathless smile.

"Good morning."

Lord have mercy, it was Troy.

"Good morning, yourself," she replied, astonished that he was there.

He held up a bag. "I thought you might like breakfast."

"Sure, sure," she said. "Come in."

He passed her but stood awkwardly at the threshold, holding his bag of goodies.

"Go all the way in, Troy. Have a seat."

He didn't immediately sit down. Instead she saw him scan the interior of her home. The furniture he noticed was eclectic and colorful; the house was warm and full of character.

"Where should I put this?" he asked, holding up a small bag.

"Whatever's in there smells good."

He smiled. "I bought fresh, warm doughnuts, hoping you would have coffee."

"Umm, you're in luck. I've got coffee already brewing. Follow me."

He followed close behind her, noticing the contours of her shapely behind in spite of the baggy sweats she wore. *Ain't nothing like a sister's booty,* he thought and smiled.

"You can put the doughnuts on this," she said, handing him a colorful ceramic platter. "I'll get the coffee mugs. You take cream and sugar?" she inquired.

"Nah, not me. I likes my coffee like my women, strong and black."

She chuckled at his comment, wondering why she wasn't offended or upset with him for coming to her house unannounced. His presence was welcome, and she hadn't even known she had wanted him to arrive.

She sat at the table across from him, her eyes danced over the mass of his forearms, the contours of his face, drinking in his mocha-colored eyes and bushy eyebrows. His nose flat and wide...a beautiful black man.

"So what brought you to my neck of the woods this morning?" she asked.

"I figured you might need some help. It's Saturday, you look like an ambitious woman. I wanted to see if I could help you with anything."

"Troy." She said his name with a smile. "We haven't even discussed your fees."

"That's it," he said, pointing his index finger at her over the rim of his cup. "You already paid for one repair."

She stared at him, perplexed. "How'd I do that?"

"You smiled."

With that comment, the laughter began between them. She was extremely flattered. He smitten.

"For real, Troy. What do you charge? I couldn't ask you to do repairs without paying for your time and expertise."

"How about if we square up at the end of the day? I'm reasonable. Trust me on that."

She watched his face for a time, tried to read his eyes and saw sincerity there. "Okay. It's a deal."

He placed the cup in its saucer, took a healthy bite of a chocolate-glazed doughnut, almost consuming it with one bite, chewed it thoughtfully while gazing at her.

It wasn't long before they were engaged in conversation, sharing tidbits about each other's lives, their respective backgrounds, siblings, schooling, and all things important, as well as inconsequential. Quips of information were shared, filtered with light laughter and gaiety. They liked each other. That was easily determined. It shone in both their eyes.

The first task he took on without her even having to ask. He noticed the railing lying haphazardly on the staircase. He put it where it belonged, somehow miraculously secured it, then asked her what else she needed.

They spent the afternoon talking to each other while listening to music between bangs of the hammer or whirling sounds coming from his electric saw or screwdriver. It seemed as if they were dancing around each other, blending easily to a melody only they could hear.

After working for hours, the house suddenly darkened as the sun swiftly disappeared behind huge, graying clouds.

"Smells like rain," Tanya said, wrinkling her nose and sniffing the air.

"Yeah, it does."

She opened a window, closed her eyes, and took slow, even breaths, her chest rising and falling in a hypnotic dance of swelling breasts softly tantalizing his senses. The coolness of the air had set her nipples erect, making Troy's mouth water.

"I love the smell of rain. It reminds me of when I was a child, and we had frequent thunderstorms and heavy rains. The scent of warm dirt and the sight of earthworms always fascinated me," she said, turning to face him. "Have you ever noticed you never see worms unless it rains?"

It took a moment for Troy to answer because he was trying to squelch the rising tide of emotions that was coursing through his loins, making his manhood throb against the zipper of his now tight jeans. Awkwardly, he cleared his throat, "I never really noticed."

"Earthworms and snails. And if you really pay attention, you can see the flowers actually opening up, as if reaching for the raindrops to settle against their delicate petals."

He thought about delicate petals and flowers opening up and each metaphor only conjured up images of her legs opening wide to receive him, and his tongue waiting to settle against the gentle folds of her sex.

"Have you ever made love in the rain?" he asked.

"What?"

"Ever made love in the rain? Lying against soft earth, a sprinkling of raindrops caressing your naked body?"

Her eyes shifted to take all of him in, and the moment she noticed the bulge, her own body began to tingle, and she felt a slow heat begin to rise between her thighs. She resisted the urge to squirm. "Uh, no. I never have."

"Would you like to?" he asked, holding his breath, hoping she wouldn't say no.

She studied him for a time, watched him observe her from across the room. "I might. Are...you...inviting me to?"

He crossed the room in quick strides, cupped her face in his hands and kissed her slow and deep, their tongues searching, probing, satisfying their hunger for each other. His hands roamed over the contours of her body, finally settling against the tautness of a nipple. Between thumb and finger, he fondled the sweet pebble. He kissed her again and groaned against her mouth as her hand stroked his throbbing dick in powerful waves of pleasure.

He led her by the hand to the privacy that awaited them in her backyard. The soft drizzle of rain greeted them, the wetness of earth tantalized and tickled their noses. With a long length of plastic laid down first, then a blanket atop that, he beckoned for her to lie down. He straddled her with another blanket hovering over his back. Warm rain and soft kisses settled all over her face, a sweet combination. She could feel the hard probing of his penis pressing against the inside of her thigh, she spread her legs wide, shuddering at his hardness—a hardness she had waited for, for far too long. His fingers searched her body, settling inside the concave deep inside her.

She was wet—wet with desire overflowing, soaking his fingers. With deliberateness he withdrew his f ingers and placed them inside his mouth—tasting her—then he explored her some more, withdrew his fingers and put them in her mouth.

She tasted herself on his fingertips, smelled her scent surround his hand, and it reminded her of the sweet smell of yeast from the days when people made bread and rolls at home from scratch. She sucked his fingers as if they were giving her life; she swirled her tongue around his hand, sucked gently, then hard, pulling his fingers into her mouth the same way she would do him once he was inside.

He fumbled with her sweatpants and unzipped his jeans. He teetered above her, teasing her, tantalizing her with the tip of him; then without warning he plunged inside. She uttered a startled cry—a mixture of joy and pain. He immediately withdrew. He did it again, this time going a bit deeper, withdrawing slowly, allowing her to enjoy the full length of him. He teased her this way for a while, enjoying the cries of delight that echoed around him, through the trees and quiet hum of raindrops. He plunged and retreated several times, each time she would thrust her hips forward to meet him in his next descent into the heavenly core of her.

At last, she began to feel him tremble as ecstasy overtook him, and she could feel his semen flowing into her body in hot, quick bursts.

"Where have you been all my life?" he whispered into her ear.

She chuckled and replied, "On the other side of town, I suspect."

"Well," he said, and kissed the tip of her earlobe, "welcome to my hood."

"For a handyman, you're very handy indeed. Do all your customers receive this kind of service?"

"Nope. Believe it or not, just you. My other customers can't hold a candle to you. Besides, you're the only woman I want to be this handy with."

They laughed.

"That's good to know," she said, while staring into his eyes. "Making love in the rain...oh that was nice. Do you think my new neighbors heard me?"

"Yep," he said. "And I bet they're all jealous."

With a smile upon her face, she closed her eyes and let the warm rain wash over her, while cradling and stroking Troy, who slept soundly in her arms.

Perfect Smile

As soon as I pulled back the heavy drapes in my darkened studio, particles of dust sprinkled and fluttered through the air, dipping and diving, creating a beautiful dance. To anyone else this would be anything but beautiful—it was, after all, just dust but I had a way of always seeing things in a different light, creating beauty where to others there simply was none. This is the nature of my work. As a photographer, my mind's eye was unique. I also believe some of my uniqueness came from being who I am—a black woman in a profession that few of us pursue. My vision, indeed my view of the world, never seemed to exactly match anyone else's, but always when my final product was unveiled and a work of art was revealed, my vision would suddenly be crystal clear to the world, and the acceptance a photographer craves would finally find its way to me.

Today, I have a photo shoot featuring a very handsome black man; the assignment was given to me in succinct detail by my agent. My photos were to show this man as being partially nude or, as she put it, the illusion of nudity, just a hint of bareness without being risqué. Her request didn't seem to be very difficult, not difficult at all, until she told me that this man was an exhibitionist, thoroughly in love with his own image. She added that if you looked up the word *nar-*

cissist in the dictionary, his picture would probably be beside it. And with those words, in my mind, the assignment changed from being ideal to being a nightmare.

As I prepared my studio for his arrival, I thought a bit about him, wondering if he deserved to be so stuck on himself. I had already made up my mind that I would not put up with any disruptive behavior, that I would immediately insist that he do as told, and I further informed myself that I would regard him with strict professionalism. In fact, I would act as if he didn't exist as anything more than just a project. I was hoping that my approach of indifference might squelch his egotistical nature.

But once he arrived, gracing the threshold of my humble studio with his powerful presence, I knew he had a genuine reason to be in love with himself. A black Adonis stood before me, so much like a mighty king that my heart skipped a beat. And everything I said I wouldn't do, I did.

I swear it seemed like several different lightning bolts struck me when I first saw him. His almond-shaped eyes shimmered as if I were gazing into a pool of pecan delight, a hint of mystery glinted behind his gaze. I became so excited by the steady and intent look on his face that I was unable to identify what about him mystified me so. He was powerful, yet while my mind quickly battled to find understanding to the source of his mystery, like a mist one moment, it was there; then it disappeared once he blinked. He broke my trance by simply smiling. And Lord, his smile was like having an unexpected ray of sunshine hit your pupils full force, a brilliance that was indescribable radiated within that smile, and for a moment I became somewhat disoriented.

His teeth were perfectly even and as bright a white as I had ever seen, as translucent as that of real pearls, precious and beautiful—perfect smile surrounding a perfect face. His chocolate-brown skin was smooth and even, uninterrupted by any flaws in tone or texture. The shape of his mouth was perfectly complemented by a well-maintained moustache and goatee. And as if this man hadn't been graced enough by impeccably good looks, it seems the good Lord also saw fit to give him one perfectly placed dimple in the center of his left cheek.

"My name's James," he said, extending his hand to me. For a moment I was transfixed, unable to comprehend that I needed to take his hand into mine and make a similar introduction. He saw my dilemma, saved me from myself, gently cradling the palm of his hand inside mine. His hand was invitingly warm, slightly callused, his grip was thoughtful, just enough pressure to entice.

"James...welcome. Come in." I finally came back to myself, felt silly and girlish and very embarrassed at my unprofessionalism. I shoved the door aside and allowed him to enter ahead of me. My goodness, the man looked as good leaving as he did coming. I closed my eyes and willed myself to settle down.

"Um...James, make yourself comfortable. We'll be shooting several different poses of you today. Um," I hedged, "several will be partially nude. I hope they told you that your photographer was female." I rushed through the sentence, sounding ridiculous even to myself.

He looked at me for a time, then he smiled, "I was hoping you would be female."

Taken aback, I said, "Why?"

"Because women and only women are able to adequately capture me on film. They," he paused, "pay attention to details."

I felt my face fill with a rush of heat. Oh, I had taken in much detail, and the lens of my camera had yet to focus on him.

"Well," I said, clapping my hands, "why don't we get started."

"Not yet," he said, stopping me with a light touch on my shoulder.

"What...what's the problem?" I stammered.

"I need two things first."

"Sure," I said. "Can I get you something to drink before we start?"

"Maybe later. What I need is a mirror—a full-length mirror—do you have one?"

I took a very deep breath, ran my hands through my hair and nervously looked around. Of course I had a mirror but that wasn't one of my props. I was tempted to tell him no, this wasn't part of my plan.

"Ahhh...yes, it's in the back, why?"

"I...make...love...to...my...self...in...the...mirror," he said, deliberately enunciating each word, leaving just enough space between them to conjure images for me. "Trust me, doing so makes for very sensual pictures."

My hand had found its way to my chest; I had started to breathe heavily. His voice and his words had me transfixed.

"I was hoping that you would make love to me," I said. Horrified. I quickly corrected myself. "I mean...not to me per se...um...to my camera. Make love to the camera," I finally said, sounding like a fool.

"Oh, I'll do that too," he said without ever taking his eyes from mine, not bothering to clarify if he meant to me or to the camera. "Where is it? I'll get it."

I pointed in the general direction of where I kept my antique floor-length mirror. He rolled it to the area I had already set up for the shoot. I had positioned studio lights for maximum effect around the room. I had a few props in place—an oscillating fan, a white sheet hanging on a rod above a bed.

"Where do you want it?" he asked.

I caught myself before I could say anything foolish. "Over to the side. I think you can see yourself but I won't catch it in the pictures," I replied.

He placed the mirror where I thought it would be the least intrusive.

"You said two things, James. What else did you need before we start?" I asked.

"Music. I must have music. Preferably jazz, lots of piano. Got any Herbie Hancock?"

"Yeah, I do. I think I've got his greatest hits. I'll go get it." I left him standing there, his eyes trailing me as I hunted for the CD. Soon the melodious sounds of the piano filled the space around us. I felt euphoric and ready to go to work on him.

Then to my utter surprise, once I had returned to where he stood, he immediately began to undress. I watched him remove his shirt in one fell swoop. He didn't bother to turn around as he unbuckled and removed his pants. He watched me as I watched him, his eyes never leaving my face. He wore canary-yellow bikini briefs that contrasted nicely with the brown tones of his milk-chocolate skin. This man had a bulge that instantly made me think of a mound of pleasure. I felt flustered but I remembered what I had been told about James, and I would not allow him to suck me into his love affair with himself.

I simply said, "Nice, very nice."

He smiled, and my stomach dipped, causing me to repress a shudder.

James turned his back to me, raised his hands above his head and grabbed the bar that held the white sheet in place. The muscles in his back bunched and bulged, veins strained against his skin, and I could see the cuts in his body—his physique one of a body builder. His bikini briefs were actually a thong, and his gluteus maximus was gloriously flawless. His skin was as smooth as velvet, and I wanted to caress his behind, just to see if it felt as good as it looked.

I placed the camera to my eye and began to take pictures of him posing this way. He heard the clicking, turned his head to acknowledge me, and then he smiled. I captured that seductive look and knew that would be one great picture. He moved his hips from side to side in a wavy, sinuous, flowing manner, simulating lovemaking to the air. I caught that sway and wished my body was pressed against his while he undulated. The backs of his thighs were muscular and when he turned the flesh over, his calves moved too. It was a mesmerizing dance of flesh and veins and skin. His body swayed as if he were a conductor in a sensual symphony. The hypnotic tones of the piano, sax, and flute flowed in and around us, completing the arousal of his lovemaking to me, himself, and my camera.

James changed his pose in one fluid motion. He sat down, legs wide apart, showing me more than I needed to see. I began to wonder how he could possibly stay contained in that small piece of yellow fabric. A fine line of hair trailed his six-packed stomach, disappeared inside his yellow briefs, making my imagination run wild. His muscular massive chest called to me. He was not covered with hair, only that beautifully sculpted, seemingly manicured, fine line of dark hair flowing down the center of his chest. I wanted to see where and how that line of hair ended. Did it lead to a much larger hairy mass or was he hairless there too, I wondered. All the while I snapped pictures of him, keeping my decadent thoughts to myself.

He spread his hands wide over his chest and began to lightly strum his fingers, moving in time with the flow of the piano we listened to, and I wished he were playing me, his fingers fluttering lightly across my breasts. He lathered his lips with his tongue, and I thought I'd die.

"Do that again," I shouted, growing excited by how a picture like that would turn out.

He looked at himself in the mirror, licked his lips slowly and provocatively. I inadvertently stepped in front of the mirror, blocking his view of himself, his eyes flickered, he focused on me and then...he did it again. A slow slathering of pink tongue against full brown lips, a sultry twinkle in his eyes, and to my utter pleasure his manhood had begun to rise.

"Show me that perfect smile," I breathlessly whispered.

And he did.

I captured in his eyes a look of decadent pleasure, and this time I was unable to suppress my desire.

"James," I said, "would you like to do some shots with your body oiled?"

"You're the photographer. Is that what you want?" he questioned, almost mocking me.

"Yes, I want. Hold on I'll get some oil." I left him sitting there with a partial hard-on, and I imagined myself slipping out of my panties, perching on his lap facing him and simply sliding down on that impressive bulge he was teasing me with.

Instead, I found the baby oil and handed it to him. He took the bottle from me, and his fingertips touched mine, lingering for a fraction of a second too long. I thought I read a message in that touch, but I wouldn't allow myself to go there even though every cell in my body screamed to be attached to him.

"Would you put the oil on my back?" he asked, handing the bottle back to me after generously lathering his chest, thighs, and legs.

"Sure," I replied, my voice high-pitched and nervous.

I poured a generous amount of the oil in my hands, rubbing them together to warm it up, then I touched him. Never even in all my imaginings would I have thought he would feel like that. So hard. So smooth. So sexy. I closed my eyes and enjoyed the feel of the velvety softness of my palm against his solid, massive back. I let my mind imagine that this was more than a photo shoot, that this was a prelude to an act that would take me to heaven. I felt, before I heard, his moans. They reverberated through the taut muscles of his back. His head hung loosely, almost touching his chest, his neck muscles strained against his skin. I massaged his back, then moved to his exposed neck, my hands flowing effortlessly across his skin.

"Hmmm," he moaned, "nice hands."

His voice was smoky, sultry, inviting, I moved my hands in a circular motion around his back, stroking him with long, firm caresses as he raised his arms above his head. It would be so easy to run my hands under his arms, around his chest and snuggle against him. Without thinking, I moved my hands around to caress his chest, the hard mounds of flesh around his pecks thrilled me. I toyed with the sculpted arch that separated his chest muscles, running my hands around his nipples, then sliding down his firm stomach and up again. With light, feathery strokes I teased him, my breath fanning the fine hairs along the nape of his neck. He shuddered. My promise to myself to never mix business with pleasure melted like the oil that disappeared against his skin. I had to stop touching him or it would definitely be on!

I moved away from him, my voice shaky and uncertain, desire wafted around me like an unseen odor—it was palatable.

I suggested that he lie down so that I could take a shot of him from an elevated angle. I wanted him to lie on his stomach and look up at me. Most of all I wanted him to smile. I stood on the chair he had been sitting on, placing it near him, close enough so I could get the shot I was aiming for. Through the lens, his slick, oiled body was magnificent. The dress I wore fluttered, and if he had a good sense of smell, I was certain he could smell me—that distinctive sweet scent of a woman.

As I towered above him, and he looked up at me and smiled, at that moment I knew that it would be very possible that this would be a picture that would gain me yet another award for photographic excellence. I muttered *ooh*s and *ahh*s while my camera clicked and whirled. I would get closer to him, then retreat; I'd stoop to my knees and circle around him, getting shots of him from every angle. His eyes would follow me, and he would twist and turn his body in ways that were purely sexual.

Without warning when I was very close to him, he turned over and pulled me atop him. I tumbled into his embrace, breathlessly shocked. He wasted no time in placing his luscious lips against mine. I wrapped my arms around him and kissed him with so much passion that I surprised myself. I could feel him rising, the bulge he had tucked away strained for release. I gyrated against him with sinuous movements while I kissed his lips, sucked his tongue, enjoying the soft pucker of his full lips against mine. I opened my legs, locking them behind his knees, lifted myself and teased him further with a slow circular motion of my wet pussy against his dick. His eyes closed, and he rocked his hips with me. I yanked my dress over my head, and he immediately unsnapped my bra, releasing my breasts, my nipples taut, ready to receive his touch. Just then the cool air from the fan swept over me, making my nipples even harder. The entrance of my womanhood throbbed. I was sensitive to touch, ready to explode. I was so wet...so ready to be seared and pounded into sweet surrender.

He stroked me through my sheer, wet panties, then pulled them to the side, not taking them off. He licked his finger, then touched me, tickling my clit with his moist fingertip. He flipped me over, snatching off my panties. He put his hands in my hair and massaged my scalp, my temples. He kissed my eyelids, cheek, forehead, and then my mouth. In my ear he whispered, "You ready for this?" And all I could do was shake my head. Yes, I was ready, had been ready since the moment I laid eyes on him.

I tugged the elastic around his waist and tore that yellow strip of fabric away from him. I could not believe what I saw then: He had been hiding himself for real! His dick was enormous and so beautiful. I've never seen a beautiful penis, but this one was. Only a slight indentation separated his head from the shaft. Otherwise it was just one long, thick, straight rod. To my utter satisfaction, he was hairless. I stroked the length of him causing a small dabble of pre-cum to surface. I wanted to lick him but before I could, he coaxed me to lie on my back.

"Me first," I heard him say, and I wasn't mad at him. *Do what ya gotta do, my brotha,* I thought.

It was my turn to be a voyeur to our actions. I watched us in the mirror. He kissed his way to my dark triangle, which throbbed and ached for the insertion of him into my warm, slick depths. His tongue worked me with such skill and expertise that I never had to instruct him to find my spot. He was immediately there, caressing me with a sensual rhythm, his pace and tempo expertly timed for maximum effect. My orgasm came so quickly that I was completely caught off guard. The inside of me grew taut then expanded, an explosion occurred, rocking the interior walls deep, deep inside of me. I felt my womb quiver and contract, the pace ebbing and flowing, strong pulsations within me swelled then finally began to weaken. My cries of delight echoed around the studio, and my whole body rocked as he continued to lick me.

He kissed the insides of my thighs as he made his way back up. He kissed my lips, and I could taste my secretions lingering there. I was quite satisfied with the foreplay. I was ready to connect with him. He kept kissing me, his tongue simulating exactly what he had done to the core of me. I was pushing myself against him wanting him to come inside. I reached for him, brushing his member back and forth. I heard him groan again; then he raised himself up. Wrapping his arms around the back of my knees, he hoisted me in the air; then he finally penetrated me. Oh, he was there, and I knew it. He long-stroked me, his movements deliberate and controlled. I watched his face and saw a mask of ecstasy there. His breath came in long puffs as he pushed himself farther into me, stroking and retreating, so I could feel every inch of him. He continued this pace for a long time, then without warning he began to pump harder and harder, pounding me into sweet surrender.

He cried out, "Yes, yes, yes. Oh, this is good," still holding my legs up, until they almost touched my ears. He trembled, kissed me again and right into my ear he whispered, "Here I cum."

I felt him expand even wider than before, his dick mercilessly stroked my G-spot, I felt like I was going to explode again.

And I did.

He finally released my legs, and I began to tremble. He watched me lose control of myself, his finger tracing lines in the pool of sweat at my navel.

"You okay?" he asked.

I couldn't speak. Instead I laughed, hysterically, embarrassed at my body's reaction to him. It was so telling, there was no way this man did not know for certain that he had rocked my world. Everything I had been told about him was not true. He was not totally into himself, and he didn't appear to have an inflated ego. I knew that from the way he made love. It was obvious that he was as interested in my satisfaction as he was in his own. And never once during our lovemaking did he peer at the mirror.

He smiled down on me—that perfect smile, that perfect body, his perfect lovemaking—and I knew then and there I wanted to see him again.

Sky-High Mind-Blowing

R ed. The color of blood, of life, of rage, of love. Her color. Shades of crimson, blue-red, orange-red, and deep burgundy lined the racks of her closet. She loved red, especially against the cinnamon tones in her skin. It was the only color that complemented the fiery coal black of her eyes and the curly ringlets in her hair. It was also the only color that made her feel especially feminine whenever she wore it, whether the color was discreetly hidden beneath her clothes, caressing, hugging, and touching her skin in the most intimate of places, or if she wore a cherry-colored dress or a powerful, bold doubled-breasted suit, the feeling was indescribable. She felt powerful in red. She could never understand why years ago red was viewed synonymously with being some sort of jezebel—a loose woman. She was neither but she knew she did have a certain inbred sexual attractiveness that she neither flaunted nor disguised. She was who she was, and whatever and however you chose to define her didn't matter one bit to her. She was proud of herself. Maya Angelou wrote about the Phenomenal Woman, and whenever Felicia heard that poem, it seemed to speak to her and her alone. She had a curve to her hips, a grace to her style, and she definitely turned a head or two whenever she swayed—not walked—into a room. She was who she was, and she liked who she was. Period.

Her lips curved into a secret seductive smile when her eyes landed on the long white box that was laid across her bed. The coat she had coveted for so long had arrived. She had eyed it daily, it seemed, in the Spiegel catalog before finally deciding to order it. It was expensive, definitely overpriced but it intrigued her, called to her. It was her style. The long box on her bed taunted her. She couldn't wait to open it. But first she had to set the mood before unveiling her most recent prized possession. She turned on the music, closed her eyes, and swayed to the saxophone of Boney James, the sweet sound caressed and soothed her mind. She headed to the kitchen and pulled her favorite crystal champagne flute—another extravagant purchase—Waterford from the coveted Millennium series, from its assigned position high on top of the shelf. She admired its beauty, plunked her finger against the glass enjoying the rich, resonating *ping that only real crystal* could make. Then she poured a full glass of Moet. She held the delicate narrow stem between two perfectly man-icured red fingertips, held it high above her head to admire the fasci-nating ascending cascade of bubbles. The tiny explosion tickled her nose as she carefully sipped the refreshing cool mixture, which left a delicate trail of delight on her tongue and down her throat. She did not want to waste a drop. Satisfied, she headed to her bedroom.

She stripped down to only her pantyhose and bra, slipped on her sexy three-inch red strappy sandals; then she opened the box. Inside the layers of tissue paper was the most exquisite coat she had ever seen. The rich texture of the fabric sung to her, felt deliciously sen-sual against her fingertips. She sighed. It was definitely worth every penny she had paid for it. It was beautiful.

The gentle caress of the fabric—rayon and brushed silk—against the warmth of her skin was somewhat electric. She felt powerful, like a sexy tigress in this candy-apple-red coat. She pranced around the room, glanced at her reflection, licked her lips, toyed with her hair, and strutted while reams of exquisite fabric fluttered around her.

The incessant ringing of the telephone pulled her out of her trance.

"Hello?" she answered breathlessly.

"What are you doing?" said the deep baritone voice of Malik, her lover.

She smiled. *Wouldn't you like to know,* she thought.. "I'm playing."

He chuckled, "With yourself?"

"Yes. I'm all alone. Would you like to join me?"

"You know I would. What exactly are you doing?"

"Admiring myself in the mirror."

She heard him suck in his breath and knew where his imagination had just taken him. Taunting him, she said, "Come play with me, Malik."

"Why don't you come to me?" he asked.

She raised an eyebrow in suspicion. "Aren't you at work?"

"Yes."

"We're obviously not on the same page, sweetheart. The kind of playing I wanna do can't be done on the job."

"Says who?" he shot back.

She laughed. "Says me!"

"Come to my office," he said seductively. "I've got something to show you."

Again she laughed. "I've already seen it, felt it, touched it, and tasted it. Why would I come all the way downtown to see what I already know?"

The bulge in his pants was becoming more and more noticeable with every word she spoke. He flinched and tried to readjust himself. Her voice, so soft and sexy and taunting, was driving him to distraction. Finally, he said, "You're killing me, Felicia. Just come down. I'll make it worth your while." He paused, then added, "I promise."

She didn't speak for a moment, too busy admiring the flash of her long brown legs peeking through the thigh-high slit of her coat. Then: "Okay. I'll come." She took a long look in the mirror. "I've got something I want to show you too."

Her preparations for the rendezvous with Malik were hurried but specific. She knew what perfumes he loved and just where to strategically place dots of the scent to enhance her own natural one. Her purpose was to create the maximum effect for any place on her body he decided to roam. And she wanted him to roam everywhere. With sweet anticipation coursing through her veins, making her heady with desire, she made her way through the deserted streets of downtown to meet Malik. She stopped at a traffic light and watched the debris bounce in a circular swirl, a tiny whirlwind, at the curb. It was windy, no sign of rain. She could usually sense when rain was coming. There would only be figurative rain showering her tonight. She smiled.

Malik moonlighted as a supervisor for a security firm. His "real" job was being a cop, a job with which she had a love-hate relationship. On the one hand she respected what he did—hey somebody had to keep the knuckleheads in check—but on the other, she worried all the time about his safety. A black man, with or without a gun, was a target as far as she was concerned. Why push the envelope?

She had mused about this too long and too hard, now realizing she had sat through two green lights. Thinking about the danger of Malik's job was starting to kill her mood until she saw the building all lit up, looming before her. The high-rise was in the heart of downtown, a location that bustled with people during the day, though at night, once the sun slipped away in the horizon of the western sky, it lost all its vigor. She parked on the street right in front of the building, a virtual impossibility during the day. The *click-clack* of her heels echoed and bounced through the archway of the entrance. She saw him right away, standing behind the information desk, a walkie-talkie pressed to his lips. He had beautiful full lips that broke into a radiant smile once he spotted her.

Felicia sauntered into the room, her fragrant perfume softly preceding her. He stared at her, his eyes never leaving her face. God she looked good all decked out in red. Her lips glistened, a fine sheen of sparkling crimson lined her mouth. Her nails and toes, he noticed, were painted red. And her coat—fabulous! He felt himself rising at the mere sight of her, anticipation made his mouth water. He licked his lips slowly, reminding her of the way L.L. Cool J mesmerizes the ladies with his decadent slather of pink tongue against full brown lips—slow, provocative, deliberate.

"Don't you look beautiful," he said, replacing the walkie-talkie in the holster at his left hip.

"Thank you," she cooed in a voice that was soft, low, sensual. "I believe you had something you wanted to show me, right?"

He didn't immediately answer her for he was captured in a trance; a state of euphoria overcame him. He felt weak.

"Malik?" she questioned, interrupting his introspection.

He cleared his throat, finally finding his voice. "Yeah, I do." He gestured for her hand, cradled it firmly inside his as they headed to the elevator.

To any passerby, they looked decent enough, like normal people waiting for an elevator but once inside the confines of that small space, he took her in his arms, inhaled deeply, and hummed a moan, the sound resonating from deep within his throat. Speaking into her hair, he said, "You smell so good, girl. Um-um-um!"

She didn't speak. She was silently enjoying the feel of his bulk in her arms and the pulsating hard beat of his heart against her cheek. Being five foot six with a man six foot two had its advantages, and this was definitely one of them. As she rested her cheek against his chest, she felt a sensation building deep within her, a slow heat rising like that of a tumultuous volcano between her thighs. With each breath she took, inhaling slowly and taking in his unique masculine scent, desire swept through her, making her dizzy with wanting.

Once they arrived on the fortieth floor, a panoramic view of the city greeted her. The city was lit up like a Christmas tree; hundreds of twinkling lights below and beyond, as far as the eye could see, lay before her like a gift. The same sparkle of the lights was reflected in her eyes as she gazed at the city she loved.

"This is beautiful," she said, exhaling breath fragrantly laced with spearmint.

"Yeah, it is, but it gets better," Malik said as he again retrieved

her hand and led her down a darkened corridor to a somewhat concealed metal door. He began to fumble with his keys.

"What's in here?" she asked.

"It's a surprise; you'll see." He paused, found the key, then
pushed open the heavy door. "Watch your step." In the darkened
space he wound his way around to yet another door. Once he
opened it, a swift gust of warm air encircled her ankles; her coat fluttered.

"Where are we?" she asked, peering around his bulk.

"The roof."

"The roof?" she repeated. "What in the world..." She stopped
short. This time she was delighted by the sight of stars that seemed
almost close enough to touch, and the moon—a half-moon—hung
low, wonderfully close to her left. Her breath caught in her throat as
she admired the beauty of the sparkling, sleeping city below.

"You like?" he asked.

"You know I do."

"This is what I wanted to show you. I found this entrance to the
rooftop by accident. The day I saw it, I knew I had to bring you here."

"Very nice," she said and turned to further admire the stars. She
held out her arms as if to embrace all the celestial bodies before her.

He matched her stance, extending his arms, intermingling his fingers with hers. He snuggled up to her, wrapped her in his arms, resting his head gently atop hers. He could smell her perfume—his
favorite—in her hair. He closed his eyes and concentrated on her at
this moment. The feel of her in his arms, the smell—her scent—
mingling with his. He could feel her pulse beating slow and rhythmically against the side of her neck where he had placed his lips. His
thumb began to trace slow, sensual circles around one of her breasts.
Her nipple stiffened, becoming as hard as a pebble against his touch.

She exhaled slowly and lazily slumped against his chest. If heav-
en could be on earth, right now it was here, forty-one stories above
the ground. Heaven, in her mind, would be to forever be held in his
arms this way. Heaven and earth sang in his embrace.

She turned to face him. "Now, it's my turn to show you something."

She sauntered away from him, the moon lighting her path. She began unbuttoning her new red coat as she walked. She turned her head and gave him an over-the-shoulder smile as she let the coat drop to the middle of her back. Her red satin bra strap seemed to beckon to him like a lover's wave. She let the coat slide farther still until he could see her almost naked hips swathed in a red silk garter belt. No panties. Her brown round behind slightly jiggled when she took a few steps; then she quickly whirled around like a model on a runway; the soft fabric of the coat whispered in the air and fell gently against her shoulder. Her sweet vee, covered in a beautiful mound of brown curls made his breath catch. A warm breeze caused her pubic hair to slightly flutter. He gasped.

Like a true vamp she walked the walk, swung her hips back and forth in a mystical dance of seduction, all the while her womanhood had his full attention. She saw he was excited; his dick throbbed and jumped against her touch. She kissed his lips while simultaneously setting him free. One warm hand traveled the interior of his pants, handled him with expertise, stroked him the way he liked to be stroked.

"You like this, baby?" she whispered.

He could not verbally respond, and it really wasn't necessary. He rose and grew with each stroke of her fingertips, firm and insistent. She was demanding his attention, and he gave it to her whether he wanted to or not. The delicate to-and-fro motion of her hand could not be denied, her power filled every pore of his soul. She forced him backward until he was against the wall.

He kissed her shoulders, gathered her face in his hands and kissed her lips. He traced the delicate fabric of her silk bra and slipped it from her shoulders, setting her beautiful breasts free. He picked her up then. She wrapped her arms around his waist, whispered in his ear, "Don't let me fall."

"Naw, baby, no way you gon' fall. I got you."

Felicia held her behind high in the air, not allowing herself to touch him yet. She wanted to control the thrust of his penetration.

She wanted to be the one to decide when and how far he went. Warm air caressed her wet pussy. She kissed his lips, sweeping her tongue slowly, seductively inside. Then she outlined the shape of his lips with her tongue. He tasted oh so familiar. She kissed his eyebrows and again used her tongue to trace its form. She used his own gesture of outlining her eyebrows with his thumb by doing so with her lips and tongue. She heard his breath being sucked in. He knew what it meant—it said "I love you."

With a comfortable ease of familiarity she finally allowed him to enter her. She was hot, slick, ready. He pushed himself in a little at a time, relishing the feel of the tip of himself inside her walls, until eventually he was fully inside her, pulsating against the delicate warmth of her womb. He felt her muscles contract around him, squeeze and release in a rhythm that matched his thrusts. He closed his eyes and threw back his head, delirious at the satisfaction coursing from her to him. He pumped and thrust as if in a well-choreographed dance with her. He held her tight in his powerful arms, tasted her lips, licked her throat, nibbled at her neck. Losing himself in her love, he rocked. His whole body trembled as he neared the brink of sweet surrender.

She felt the change in his thrust, and she heard the growl that was beginning to form at the back of his throat. He was ready to come. Abruptly, she stopped moving, yanked herself from him, unraveled her legs from his waist, forcing him to put her down.

"Not yet, baby...not yet," she said.

He was stunned.

She turned her back to him and again raised her behind in the air, stood on her tiptoes, and urged him to enter her from behind. Quickly he resumed his coveted position inside her. She grabbed the rail and bucked against him with wild thrusts. He fingered her clit with his wet fingertip, flicked it back and forth, matching the thrusts of their hips. He heard her breath coming harsh and quick, her breasts dangled and bounced, hitting the concrete wall. The thought that she might be hurting herself came to him, so he held and fondled both her breasts with one hand, while the other tickled her clit.

She felt his hand protecting her, they were hot and sweaty, but this was not where she wanted his hand to be. She moved them both to surround her butt. He forced her cheeks open and plunged deeper. They were almost in a sitting position, the backs of her thighs, rested softly against him. A slice of pain overtook her as he went deeper and deeper inside her. The color red clouded her vision; she closed her eyes even tighter, and her mind saw red flames framing his face as his seed began to spill from his loins into her cocoon.

They came together in a rush of warm heat and friction. Their collective screams of delight were lost, swiftly carried away with the sound of the wind.

Finally they collapsed, laughing at their little escapade.

"Where'd you get that coat?" he asked.

"You bought it for me, honey, don't you remember?" she said, an innocent look on her face.

"It's nice," he replied, knowing he had nothing to do with the purchase.

He kissed the side of her face and pulled her closer to him. "Do you think you would come to me this way if you weren't my wife?"

She laughed. "I'm much more than your wife, I am your lover, the woman you chose to fulfill your every fantasy."

"I don't have fantasies, Felicia," he said with a light chuckle.

"Yes, you do. Everybody does."

"Not me," he insisted.

"You never fantasized about a beautiful woman, clad in next to nothing, coming up to you, wrapping her naked self around you, and fucking your brains out with wild abandon...never?" she asked, her eyebrow perched questioningly.

"Hmm," he said. "It was nice."

"It was better than nice, and you know it. It was nothing short of sky-high mind-blowing."

"Yeah it was. Keep on blowing my mind, baby. Keep on blowing my mind."

Much later he watched his woman in red sashay away. This woman—his woman—was a seductress. His red-deviled lady left a strong impression on his mind, upon his heart, and a wonderful trail of her scent upon his fingertips.

You, He, and Me

I love to dance. I can dance till I sweat so hard my hair frizzes up tighter than tight. Unfortunately, I do not get an opportunity to dance like this because where I live all the brothers are stuck on white girls, or as close to white as they can get, completely leaving chocolate sisters like me out of the loop. I would go to the local black clubs and sit and sit, sipping on the same drink all night long, hardly ever getting asked to dance. One day one of my girlfriends invited me to go party with her at a gay/lesbian bar. I had absolutely no desire to do that, but she told me I would get to dance, and no one cared if I chose to dance alone. After a brief moment of hesitation, I agreed to go.

My hesitation in going was more out of fear of attracting someone of my same sex, and that was not my reason for going there. I considered myself to be straight, and I did not want to offend anyone, and certainly not on their own turf—in one of their own clubs. But the desire to dance overtook all my misgivings.

We arrived at the club, which was situated on the outskirts of town, and from the parking lot I could hear the music thumping and bumping. Once inside, the bass reverberated inside the walls of my chest, and I knew this was where I wanted to be. The music was like an aphrodisiac, making me feel high and very sexy. My friend could see that I was shimmying and bouncing in my seat. She playfully pulled me onto the dance floor. The music took over, and I swayed and rocked my hips to the beat. It was extremely dark in this club, so dark that I could barely see my friend's face. But I could feel the music in and around me; I closed my eyes and rocked to one song after another.

We were drinking Long Island Iced Teas, and before I finished drink number one, another one arrived, and my head began to swim. I lost all my inhibitions, repeatedly heading to the dance floor unescorted every time I had a mind to. Liquor and good music make me feel so sexual. I wanted to slide up to someone and rock my hips against them.

Then from across the dance floor standing beside the ladies' room, I saw him. He stood against the wall, the light from the opening and closing door giving me a good view of his face. He had a body that couldn't be denied. He wore a black muscle T-shirt and black jeans that hung low off his hips. He had a huge bulge that I could see from where I stood checking him out. He would do nicely. I circled the room like a woman in heat, keeping my eye on him. He must have sensed my presence. He watched me too. He pushed himself from the wall and began to advance toward me. We met in the center of the room. At that moment no one else existed but me and him. He reached for my hand and together we headed to the dance floor. Our timing couldn't have been better, for as soon as we stepped on the smooth parquet, a slow jam began to play, as if it had been selected for us. He pulled me close, locked his thigh securely between both of mine, and I began to rock, riding his muscular thigh.

"What's your name?" he finally asked.

"Whatever you want it to be, partner," I replied.

He laughed, a sexy low rumble in my ear, then told me his name was John.

Frankly I didn't care what his name was. I had an agenda, and it was twofold: First I wanted to dance till the soles of my feet throbbed, and then I wanted to make love. At that moment loving a complete stranger was okay with me too.

"Have you ever been here before?" he asked me.

"Nope, first time."

He said nothing for a time. We rubbed and teased each other, he stroked my thighs, lightly grazed my breast with his hand. We were simulating intercourse vertically in the darkness of this club. He leaned forward and right in my ear he said, "There's a special room here, if you're interested."

"What kind of room?" I asked and stepped back to peer into his face.

"A room you can play in."

"Ahh," I said, finally figuring out what he was talking about. He took my hand in that darkened place and held it against himself. He had a serious hard-on, and I could feel him throbbing.

"Okay," I said, agreeing far too quickly to go with him.

Actually there were several special rooms. And the first of my five senses that awakened once we entered the narrow hallway that led to the rooms, was my sense of smell. I could smell sex—hot sex— coming through the walls like someone's pores. I could hear muffled moans and groans here and there, and it turned me on the same way watching a porn flick does. We ended up in a room that wasn't occupied. A nice full-size bed and nightstand were all that were in there. That's all we needed.

He kissed me, and I felt that familiar rise of sexual expectation begin to course through my veins. Against his mouth I asked him, "You got any condoms?"

"Yes. Safety first, right?"

"Right," I replied seriously.

"I wanna lick you—lick you and drown that little man in the boat."

My breath caught. Yes, I would definitely like that. But I was losing my perspective so I chose to deliberately walk away from him. When I turned around, he was eyeing my sistah-girl booty and wide hips.

"You sure you want to do that?" I asked him.

"It's your call. Frankly, I'd rather taste before I stick." He unzipped his pants then pulled his enormous member out and let it dangle semi-hard outside his pants.

I gasped. "Lord, have mercy," I said. "What the hell are you packing?"

"Nine soft, about ten and a half hard. Can you hang?"

Hmm, I thought, *let me rethink this.* The little hard-on I had for him was quickly deflating as I openly stared at him. Homeboy looked like he could hurt somebody, and I am not into pain.

Just when I was about to change my mind, this beautiful black woman walked in with an innocent lost look on her face. She was about five-foot-three or-four, had honey-colored skin and short brown hair with blond streaks that almost matched the tones in her skin. She had dark, smoldering eyes, a wide nose, and she wore very little makeup.

"Excuse me. I'm sorry, I've got the wrong room," she said in a soft voice, turning to leave.

"No," I shouted. "Don't go. This could be the right room," I said, hedging. All of a sudden I wasn't sure I wanted to be left alone with this man.

To this day I do not know why I said that. A ménage á trois was never in my plans for that night. All I had originally wanted to do was dance. Her unexpected arrival gave me a little time to decide whether or not I was going to get it on with this man.

"Yeah," he said, turning his attention to her. "Come in and join us."

I remember now that she never really looked at him—her full attention seemed to be on me. That was cool, because I was feeling so conflicted then, I didn't care that she seemed to be checking me out. Maybe she could save me from myself.

"Y'all wanna do this or what?" he asked, making me turn my attention back to him.

I took a deep breath, looked from him back to her and truly did not know what to say. He was fine—yes, he was definitely fine—and even though I knew exactly why I had followed him to this room, I wondered if I wanted to try to handle all he had to offer. That was a serious question that I needed to ponder some more. Maybe if I had another drink I could do this.

"You got something to get my head nice?" I asked.

"No drugs, baby, just sex, that's our drug."

"No, I meant liquor. Can we get a drink back here?"

He sighed like he was getting quite exasperated with me. "Yeah, what do you want? I'll go get it."

At the same time we both shouted, "Hennessey, water back."

I looked at her again and together we began to laugh. It was nervous laughter. We both had the jitters it seemed.

He left, slamming the door behind him. I heard him mumble something under his breath but I didn't care what he said because I was busy looking at her, trying to figure out why she was back here.

"So, what's a nice wholesome-looking woman like yourself doing in a place like this?" I asked.

"Curiosity."

"Yeah," I chimed in. "Curiosity killed the cat."

"Satisfaction brought him back," she replied, ending the familiar saying.

Again we laughed. She had a sweet, infectious laugh, and she was pretty. Too pretty to be here, I thought. My assessment of her made me think about myself. Don't get me wrong, I'm no slouch, but pretty did not exactly describe me. I had a bit of a hard edge. Life had kicked my behind a time or two, and that fact had a way of showing on my thirty-five-year-old face.

"You looked scared when I came in," she said.

I averted my gaze and mumbled an affirmative "yeah," while nodding my head.

"What scared you?" she asked.

"Him," I said, gesturing in the direction of the closed door.

"Why?"

"Let's just say he fits all the rumors you've ever heard about the well-endowed black man."

"Oh," she replied. "I didn't notice. I only saw you."

She started to approach me. She seemed to be looking past me, peering over my shoulder. Just when I was about to turn to see what she was looking at, she swatted at something near my left ear.

"Spider," she said.

I could smell her perfume; it was powerfully subtle.

"What's the name of the perfume you're wearing?" I asked. She was still standing right next to me. She seemed to be studying my face.

"Irish Spring," she replied with a seriousness that surprised me. She blinked several times in quick succession, and then she threw back her head and laughed like she had just told the best joke ever.

I laughed with her, but it wasn't that funny. I had simply become involved because of the infectious nature of her laughter. She touched my face then. Her hand was small, her nails short, absent of any nail polish I noticed. I didn't understand the gesture, and I didn't know how to react to it, but it felt nice.

There was a knock on the door, which made us both jump like guilty children engaged in conduct we shouldn't have been.

"Two Hennesseys with water backs," he announced as he entered carrying a tray with two small brandy snifters and two tall glasses of ice water with red straws.

"Thanks," we both said, again in unison.

I grabbed my glass wanting to knock the drink back in one swallow but I didn't. Hennessey is not for guzzling. Cognac is the kind of drink you savor slowly like a lover's kiss. But I was nervous, in need of a quick jolt that would calm me down.

I felt her soft hand again. This time she was pulling me toward the bed where he was already waiting—naked—his very large member resting dangerously against his inner thigh.

"Ladies, let's do this!" he commanded.

I stared at her, and she stared at me. I couldn't believe what was happening but I did nothing to stop it. She began to undress me, pulling my one-piece dress over my head. I hadn't worn a bra—in fact I hardly ever did unless I had to. She seemed to like my breasts, she didn't resist touching them. I felt an electric current from her touch against my bare skin, against my breasts. Her hand was so soft, as soft as mine. It didn't feel like I thought it would. A woman's

44

hand caressing me in a sexual manner, I thought would feel repulsive, unwelcome. But I was wrong.

She toyed with the waistband of my panties, her fingertips lightly brushing the top of my pubic hair, while she cuddled and fondled my breasts. My nipples instantly responded to her caress, which was as soft as a whisper. A moan escaped me before I had a chance to stifle it. I felt relaxed, and I was now extremely horny. She began to tug at my panties, which didn't immediately fall. I had on a thong, and it was securely trapped inside my butt cheeks. She urged me to spread my legs, which I did, and they easily came down with the next tug.

Before I knew it, I was undressing her, touching her breasts, trailing my hand down a path that led to her firm abdomen. She was hairless. She had a tattoo where hair should have been. I marveled at that tattoo and what was behind it.

We somehow found ourselves on each side of the bed. He was as happy as a pig in slop, smiling broadly as his flaccid penis began to rise. She rarely even looked at him—it was as if he didn't exist. He reached up and fondled one of her breasts and one of mine. She reached for me, wanting to touch my soft, curly mound and my clit, which was protruding from my hairy mass. I followed her lead and did the same. I had never touched a woman—never. This forbidden act did not feel wrong at all. How in the world it felt right is beyond me, but it did, it most certainly did.

I touched her skin where her tattoo was. It was a snake that appeared to wrap around, as if ready to squeeze her clit or strike anyone who approached the area. It mesmerized me in more ways than one. I stared at her body, then into her eyes. *What in the world am I doing,* my mind shouted, but I let her touch me—as I touched her—and—he touched both of us.

He grabbed my hips and coaxed me to straddle him, she took her place behind his head. Still she stared at me. I knew what I was doing with him, but I wasn't too sure about what would happen with her. I leaned forward, and he took one of my double Ds in his mouth. He sucked a little too hard, and I gasped, closing my eyes. Then I felt lips—her lips—on mine. She kissed me with a sweet tenderness that made my heart stand still as if I had waited all my life for this kind of kiss. Her tongue timidly probed my mouth; she swirled it around, tracing my lips and their form with the tip of her tongue. I tasted cognac. I kept my eyes closed, not wanting anything to break my concentration of this sensation. A woman's lips. Nice...very nice.

I felt fingers probing me—large fingers—trying to get inside of me. I opened my legs wide, and with his guidance I slipped down onto him, very slowly. All the while she was kissing me, touching my breasts and fondling my clit. Oh, Lord, I wanted to scream. This was ecstasy at its highest. I moved sensuously up and down on him until I had most of him inside me. I opened my eyes to see that she was now straddling his face, and he was licking her while her hips rocked. She began to moan, her breath against my mouth, inside my mouth, I heard her groan. Then so did I. She placed her entire hand over me, rubbing my clit with the soft palm in a rhythm that seemed to match the rocking of her hips against him. Oh, my excitement was building, reaching higher and higher. I almost couldn't stand any-more. I was on the brink of coming. I threw back my head and rode all ten inches of him like a wild woman possessed. I arched, leaned way back, grabbed my ankles, and bucked. I felt his dick stroking my sensitive G-spot. Yessssss. I could actually feel my clit growing. It pulsated, filling up with blood as my orgasm began to build.

The first flicker of her tongue caught me by surprise. It was hot and urgent and deliciously sensuous. Her exploration of me was complete, I could only describe it as knowing. She knew how to suck me, she knew how to stroke me, she knew how hard and how soft to apply pressure. She also could keep up a consistent rhythm that most men are unable or unwilling to do.

"Oh, gawd," I screamed. An explosion happened inside my head, causing my body to quiver and shake. My nipples tightened into two taut little pebbles, a series of goose bumps raced up and down my arms. Sweat trickled down my spine, giving me a slight chill. And then the spasms began. Like a tiny marching band around the most sensitive part of me, I contracted. I held my breath and felt my pulse racing, I heard ringing in my ears. These delicious few seconds turned me on, and they turned me out.

"Ahhh," I growled.

It was then that I realized she was the one who had made me cum so hard and so strong. It was her presence that did me in. I could feel him inside of me but it had started to hurt, the thick latex was beginning to irritate me. Suddenly, I wanted things to change. I wanted the impossible. I wanted to somehow become one with her. I wanted to be inside of her, exploring the essence of her being. I wanted to know how she tasted, my fingers wanted to knead her flesh, stroke her inner thighs, I wanted to extract nectar from her loins. I wanted my tongue wrapped around that snake. I reached for her face with both hands. I kissed her, tasting my own juices upon her lips. I stopped thrusting—the man below me no longer existed. At that moment it was only me and her. And it was on!

I lost all my inhibitions as I stroked her everywhere. I ran my fingers through her hair, I suckled her breasts like a newborn baby wishing milk would come and satisfy my thirst. I clutched her buttocks, pulling her away from his gaping mouth. I rolled him over. He probably thought I intended to do something freaky from behind. Wrong! I gently laid her down, got between her legs, wishing with all my might for a connection. But when the connection happened, I was startled because it wasn't that we connected with our bodies, we had somehow managed to connect with our minds. She whispered sweet words to me.

"You make me want to go there," I heard her whisper. "Do you want me to go there?"

"Yes."

"You are one of the most beautiful women I've ever seen," she said. "I see your beauty in your eyes. You can't hide. In your eyes I can see so much."

Before I realized I had gotten so emotional, one of my tears hit her cheek and splattered, leaving a wet track down the side of her face. She did not even attempt to wipe it away.

"No one has ever told me that," I said, my voice choking as I spoke.

"The moment I saw you in this room with him," she said, gesturing, "I knew you needed me and not just for this."

"What exactly is it you think I need?" I whispered timidly, afraid to hear her answer.

"Love."

And you know what, she was right. I did need love, and I needed acceptance, and from her I have received both. I fell in love with her that night. So now I know two things: One, you can fall in love at first sight and two, it can happen just from that person's touch or her tender words.

We dance together all the time, and I never feel ashamed or alone since now I'm proudly loving her.

Unfinished Business

Derek watched her in the darkness of the smoke-filled club as she approached the stage; the sway of her hips mesmerzing him in a way that no other woman's could. He smiled in the darkness, happy that she was there tonight, ready to read her sensuous poetry to a large crowd of people. He noticed the thigh-high split on the side of the black ankle-length dress she wore. Her calves flexed as she glided regally across the room in four-inch suede shoes. Her legs emphasized and made even more beautiful (if that were possible) by sheer black hosiery. He uttered a secret sigh as he remembered the last time she had performed a very private poetry reading for him and him alone.

"Good evening. It's so wonderful to see so many poetry lovers here tonight. My name is Nikki, and for the next half hour, I'm going to take you on a poetic journey. Y'all ready to ride!" she shouted, and the crowd went crazy, the applause loud and strong.

Once the deafening noise began to subside and the lights receded, she took everyone from one magical tale to another. He knew she would talk of good love, unrequited love, being black in America, and that she would read philosophical, political poetry that would leave everyone in the audience in awe. Derek could hear her voice as he watched her, but his mind had floated away, remembering another day some time ago when he had Nikki all to himself...

They were outside in a parking lot of the movie theater discussing the intricate details of the movie they had just seen. She seemed very happy that day. She played with him, teased him, and flirted with him in her own special way. He was leaning against the car, his legs crossed at the ankle, staring at her as she gestured and wiggled her hips to emphasize a point she was making. He didn't know that on his face he held an expression that made her stop abruptly.

"What?" she inquired of him with raised eyebrows.

"Nothing," he replied. "I'm just listening to you."

"You've got a goofy look on your face. What's up with that?" she asked and smiled, moving closer to him.

"Me, a goofy look. Nah, baby, not me. I was just watching you wiggle your hips. Trying to turn a brotha on," he joked.

She slapped at him, playfully tapping his shoulder. "I am not trying to turn a brotha on. I was just talking!"

The tone of her voice, he noticed, was not at all antagonistic or confrontational. She was just being Nikki.

"Maybe," he paused. "Simply being in your company turns me on. Just stop wiggling okay, you're making things rise."

With no shame at all she looked at his crotch, finally noticing the bulge that had begun to strain against the button fly of his Levi's.

"Ummm," she said and licked her lips provocatively. "Should I do my Mae West impression?" She placed her hands on her hips and swayed back and forth, puckered her lips and blew a kiss to the wind. Then: "Is that a pickle in your pocket, or are you glad to see me," she drawled using a bad Southern accent.

He laughed at her—a low guttural sound, shaking his head. He was embarrassed, for she had an effect on him that he could not suppress or deny. He placed his hands in front to hide himself.

"Don't do that, big boy," she continued, placing her small hands against his, gently tugging at them. "Let me see what a brotha got."

With a suddenness that surprised both of them, he remembered, he grabbed her, pulled her into his arms, settling her against his rising mound, both his hands on her butt, cradling her firmly. He kissed the side of her face and neck. "I've been wanting to do that all day."

She moved, lightly grinding herself against him. "Ummm," she muttered again. "Don't start none, won't be none," she whispered in his ear.

"Too late," he said as he stared into her eyes for a long time. "You don't know what you do to me, girl. Every time I see you, you do things that make me want you."

"Things," she uttered, "like what?"

"Like your voice and the way you read poetry. Damn girl. You have all the men wanting you with that sensual voice."

She swayed in his arms a little. "I just finished a new poem. Want to be the first to hear it?"

"Hell yeah," he enthusiastically replied.

She kissed his cheek; then against the softness of his ear she whispered, "Read poetry to me, baby, while I lie in your arms, grab a book and...read poetry to me." Her tone was soft, beckoning him to follow her wherever she led him. " 'Cause listening to your voice makes me want to scream," she continued. "I want to hear it echo off the walls of your chest." She stopped and caressed his chest through the thin fabric of his shirt. "The one I'm aching to caress. I want to hear you read, baby...read poetry to me."

She loosened his grip on her waist and settled more deliberately against his growing mound. She opened her legs wider, spooning her feminine softness against him.

"While I straddle your lap and you croon in my ear, words sweet and tender in rhyme and verse in complete unison with the gyrations of my hips," she swayed provocatively against him, pressing her softness against his hardness. "Read poetry to me so I can watch your thick, sexy lips move." She took the tip of her finger and traced a delicate outline of his lips. "And every now and again your tongue appears to," she paused, "lick and quench those luscious lips while words that delight spill like pearls dropping one by one, finding their way to my heart."

He licked the tip of her finger, waiting for her to continue.

She could feel him growing larger, straining against his jeans as if he were about to burst. She took her hand and cupped him. "Stroke my soul with gentle breezes," with expert hands she applied pressure. "Feed me visions of love...good love...tales of harmony and ecstasy blending effortlessly as you read poetry to me." Overcome with desire, she rested her lips against the side of his neck and sighed. "I want to hear you read, baby...read poetry to me," she whispered in finality.

With a suddenness that surprised both of them, she pushed herself away from him, pushing out her bottom lip. "Shoot, Derek, I can't remember the rest."

Then she burst out laughing, leaning away from him. "I think I even messed up that last line."

"Nikki, why'd you do that to me?" he asked her, speaking in low tones, his voice husky and filled with desire. He still held her even though she was now an arm's length away. The warmness of her body next to his was seeping away with the light breeze that he noticed was now tousling her hair.

"I thought you'd like it. Did I do something wrong?" she asked, searching his face.

He shook his head as if attempting to ward off a trance. "I'm trying to stay celibate, Nikki, but you're making a brotha weak, lose all his resolve."

He saw embarrassment streak her face. "Oh. I'm sorry," was all she uttered.

He remembered now how that awkward moment between them seemed to last an eternity. Neither one of them knew what to say. Finally he said, "It's okay. You ready to head home?"

That date, their first real date, ended with her feeling rejected. He knew that because she didn't say another word. They drove in silence. But he wasn't rejecting her, not at all. What he was trying to do at that point in time was something he needed to do for himself. He wished it had been another time, space, and place so everything he felt for her could have come to fruition that day. He wanted to do more than "read poetry to her." He had no doubt in his mind about that!

His introspection was interrupted by the strong echo of her voice as she began to end yet another powerful piece of poetry. The crowd had erupted in loud clapping, and people began to stand all around him. An ovation for her.

After her performance Derek stood back, partially hidden by the comfortable darkness of the club. He watched as a number of people praised her, thanked her, asked her questions about the power of her poetry. They shook her hand, hugged her, and some even kissed her. The emotion that she had stirred within them was something they had to release, like the awakening of the sun upon your face. You just had to tell someone about that experience. She took all the comments in with a graciousness that was soothing, her humility undaunted, her inner peace was as powerful as her words. Finally, she was almost alone, only one person remained talking to her. He approached her from behind.

"You were fantastic tonight, as usual," he said.

She turned to find him standing there all smiles with his arms opened wide. She looked surprised; then her smile appeared as joy rested in her eyes. She stepped into his arms without a word. He held her against his chest, a slight tremble within him told both of them a lot. He was not only nervous, but he realized then that he had worried about whether or not she would accept him after so much time had passed, and there were so many questions still unanswered.

"How have you been, Nikki?" he finally asked, releasing her.

"Okay. How 'bout you?"

"I'm better now...now that I've seen you."

"Where have you been hiding?" she asked him, noticing how different he looked. His beautiful sun-kissed brown skin was still smooth, and now he had shaved his head. His skull seemed perfectly sculpted, and it looked glossy.

"You look good, Derek...real good," she said with a smile.

She continued to check him out, admiring the light brown of his skin, the fullness of his lips. She wished he didn't have a ring piercing the tender flesh of his bottom lip, but he did. When he talked, she could also see a flash of silver that skewered the soft pink of his tongue . And even though she didn't understand his desire to adorn himself this way, she had to admit that it added to his uniqueness—his sexual appeal. His smile was mischievous and inviting...so inviting.

He blushed at the compliment, slightly bowed his head and lowered his eyes. He smiled. "Thank you. And you look as good as usual."

"I've missed you," she said.

And with those words a stirring began deep within his soul. His eyes searched her face. He had so much to tell her, to share with her.

"Can we go somewhere and talk?"

"Sure," came her ready reply. "Let me get my things together. I'll meet you at the exit."

His mind began to replay the rehearsed things he wanted to say to her. Most of all he wanted her to know his dry spell was over, and if she would allow it, he wanted to make love to her. He had solved some issues in his mind, and he was ready to be with a woman again. And more than anything he wanted to be with her.

Nikki felt giddy with excitement. It had been so long since she had seen Derek. Their last date was fun but ended awkwardly. She'd thought he wanted her, but she had been wrong. She was embarrassed, felt silly for pushing herself on him that way. Normally, that wasn't even her style, but she thought he was giving her the signals, and she was willing—more than willing—to let him come inside, stay for a while, until they were both satisfied.

That was then; this was now.

She found him standing outside the club, his alert brown eyes darting here and there, taking in all the sights and sounds of an almost vacant downtown. It seemed that no matter how much the city tried to revitalize downtown, people were just not really buying it. If they had specific business in that area, they came at night, but if not, it was still a place that was virtually deserted after six o'clock.

"Derek?" she called his name, almost not willing to disturb his thoughts. He turned toward the sound of her voice and immediately upon seeing her, he smiled.

"Hey, beautiful."

"I thought you had left town or something. I haven't seen you in a long, long time."

"No, I've been around, just chillin' at the house, workin', thinkin'..."

"Thinking," she interrupted. "About what?"

"Lots of things...and you."

"Me!" she said, astounded.

"Yeah, you. I couldn't quite face you after what happened the last time we were together."

"What happened then, Derek? I felt so stupid. I read you wrong, didn't I?"

"Nope, you didn't. I wanted you so bad that day, but my life wasn't straight, and I cared too much about you to drag you into my nightmare. But..." he paused, "my nightmare is over. I'm in the light now, and I want to see if you and I can kick it again some time."

"Don't get me wrong Derek. I'm really glad to see you, but you've got some explaining to do, don't you think?"

"You're right," he said, taking her hand inside his own. "In a nutshell, I had lots of things going on back then. I was involved with a lady who had some serious problems and I was trying to be her hero—her savior. And..." He paused. "Well, let's just say it didn't work. I couldn't save her; she had to save herself.

"I got really depressed, started drinking too much, partying harder than I ever had before, had a bad attitude about women. Then I started hanging around some white boys at work, got drunk, went to a tattoo parlor, got an expensive-ass tattoo," he stopped to show her the six-inch hump on his bicep where a beautiful tiger graced his arm. "And then I did the piercings on a stupid dare. I guess I was sort of lost for a while, trying to find myself, get over my pain.

"When I met you, I thought you were so beautiful and smart, and you made me think about stuff I had stopped thinking about—caring about. It wasn't just your poetry that affected me, it was you. The more time I spent with you, the more I missed being part of a relationship—a healthy relationship. But I knew I couldn't step to you right. Not then anyway."

Nikki didn't speak for a time, just watched him as he stared into her eyes. "But you're okay now?"

"Yes, my wild days are over."

"You went a little crazy with the piercings, I see."

He stuck out his tongue at her, toyed with the silver prong. "Yeah, I guess so. But even though they seem weird, women really are intrigued by them. I can't tell you how many women openly tell me they would like to know how this silver ring feels while caressing her tongue or grazing the tender core between her legs."

"Really," she said, squirming just a bit at the image that sprang to her mind. "Intriguing, hmm…"

"Nikki, I want you to read to me. Read poetry to me."

She smiled, shaking her head at the memory of the night she recited that poem to him.

"Nikki, can I ask you a question?"

"Yeah."

"How do you kiss?"

"What?" she said with genuine surprise.

"How do you kiss? I listen to your voice and watch you walk and when you talk your lips just…ummm…they do things to me. I want to know how they feel. Can you kiss?"

"Of course I can kiss."

"Let me see."

For a while she said nothing, did nothing. Her mind was quickly trying to assess and accept the things he had just told her. "Derek, what do you think this is? I haven't seen you in months; then you waltz back into my life all pierced up and asking for kisses."

"You know why I'm asking for a kiss?"

"No," she said. "Why?"

"Because you and I have some unfinished business, Nikki. Please let me show you what I couldn't before."

He smiled again, and again she saw the glimmer of that silver spike in his tongue, and her body wanted to know what it felt like.

She wanted to experience that sensation against the sticky warmth of her clit.

So it began on a warm spring night, on the corner of Fifty-Second and Broadway; she entered the tender embrace of Derek, and for the first time tasted a little bit of heaven.

He kissed her softly, his lips melding against hers in sensual surrender. She could feel the ring that penetrated his bottom lip, and at first it was really strange. She was uncertain as to how to react to it. He kissed her closed-mouth with a butterfly-type motion, teasing her, testing her, arousing her, moving to her throat, the side of her jaw, her cheeks, closed eyelids, then back to her mouth. Then he stopped toying with her lips, pushed his tongue inside the warm contours of her mouth to begin suckling her tongue. The sensation of metal was exciting and erotic as he swirled and swept around her mouth until she could feel her panties were wet, and she was ready for more— much more. She returned his kisses, toyed with the ring in his bottom lip, sensuously darting the tip of her tongue in and out of it.

Once he finally pulled away from her, Nikki wiped away the lipstick that had been smeared all over his face and lips.

"That's a good color for you," she teased, while lightly stroking his lips with her fingertips, swiping away the evidence of their kiss.

He whispered, "You remember where I live, right?"

She stopped mid-stroke and simply nodded.

"Meet me there."

The minute she entered his apartment, he kissed her with renewed intensity as he began to undress her. The room was mostly dark except for one lit scented candle. Just before her eyes completely closed, she glimpsed the silvery shadow of the moon's light shining through the ceiling's skylight.

She sighed as she felt his fingers slip inside the elastic of her panties, sliding them down the length of her legs. She still had on high heels. She didn't want to fall, so she grabbed his head—so soft, smooth, and bald—to steady herself as she stepped out of her panties. He obviously took this as a signal, for he immediately buried his face between her legs, his tongue parting and exploring the lining of her feminine lips. Warm hands caressed and stroked her calves—the same calves he had admired so much earlier that evening.

The sighs and purrs that escaped from her were like music to his ears, a chorus of desire escaping her throat, filling the room with sounds of ecstasy. Intense heat came from his hands as they continued to explore her legs, finding their way up the backs of her thighs, settling on the roundness of her butt. He licked her. Repeatedly the round tip of the silver tongue ring grazed her clit, raising her desire to new heights. She felt his fingers as he explored her from behind. Mercilessly rhythmic, he licked her while fingering her, one finger grazed inside her and one finger explored the entrance to her anus. Her toes curled, and she wished she was out of her shoes so she could grip the carpet with her bare feet.

She teetered on the edge of total abandon. She breathed deeply and silently through her nose, her concentration intense. She tumbled, falling into her orgasm, her whole body retracting and seizing. She bucked against his face, her nails dug into his head as sweat trickled down her spine, and her nipples grew taut. The muscles of her legs quivered almost in unison with the contractions that pumped through her, hard and strong.

"Oh, God," she screamed. "Derek, I'm going to fall."

He swooped her up, carried her to his bed and without further hesitation, he entered her. With deliberate care, he inserted himself deep inside of her, then quickly retreated. She felt something different, a sensation that was totally foreign-new to her.

"What...is...that..." she haltingly said, her voice raw.

He gently glided himself inside her again. "My dick is pierced too. You like?"

"Oh...God...oh...oh...ohhhhh," she muttered as he continued to enter her, then retreat. The underside of him was double pierced so she could feel the arousing pressure on the base of her vaginal wall. The piercing sent delicious sensations running through her. His strokes were strong and sure…heaven. He stopped pushing himself inside of her because he could feel her sucking him in, pulling him deep inside her wetness, a welcome intrusion. She dug in her heels and used her muscles to push him over the edge. Doing those kegel exercises paid off now more than ever before.

"Oh, baby, I'm cumming," he said, his voice urgent.

"Ahh, yes," she said. "Come on, baby, I'm ready."

He didn't move. His whole body, even his breathing stopped. Nikki could feel him expanding horizontally inside her, stretching her wide. Then she felt his release pressing hard against her G-spot, squirting torrents against her sensitive area. She felt herself stirring again, the pressure building and building.

"Oh, Lord," she breathed. "I'm going to come again."

And she did. A surprising amount of liquid burst forth from her, mingling with his juices. Her chest felt tight as she clutched him, riding the wave of orgasmic ecstasy. His sweat dripped on to her like a waterfall, leaving petals of wetness on her breasts. It felt like warm rain, and suddenly she wanted to cry tears of joy, of happiness, releasing every pent-up emotion she felt for Derek. Her tears fell, mingled with sweat and his sweet kisses.

He watched her, intent upon understanding the emotions tumbling from her. He felt it, too, but he would never cry, although his heart was full right now. Full of satisfaction and desire and maybe even love.

Their unfinished business was still not complete as far as he was concerned. He still had much, much more to say.

And he hoped they still had time and energy to embark upon Round Number Two. Then they would talk some more.

I Missed You

*H*e calls her every now and then, perhaps just to hear her voice. She's never really sure. They exchange polite pleasantries and seem to ask all the right questions of each other. How are the boys? she asks. Then, he dutifully inquires about her grown children, how things are going for each of them at college, etc., etc. Then, a quiet softness blankets them. Neither knows what else to say. This time she decides to take a bold step and just ask him what she wants to know.

"Do you miss me?" she whispers.

"Maybe," he answers.

She laughs, even though she is not pleased that he doesn't really know. "You're not giving up anything, are you? After all this time, you still won't say it, will you?"

He responds with a slight chuckle of his own, then, "I just wanted to call to see how you're doing. How are you doing?"

"I'm fine," she replies.

"Anything exciting happening in your life?" he asks.

"Not really. Why do you ask?"

"Just curious."

"If you're asking me if I have a man in my life—"

"I'm not asking you that," he interrupts. "Look, I just wanted to

60

say hello, not argue."

"Who's arguing?" she quips.

There is a long pause.

"If I get some time this evening, I'll call you at home. Okay?"

"Of course," she replies, knowing he wouldn't.

This has become a familiar catch-all phrase he uses every time he calls her. I'll call you...later. But later never seems to come. She replaces the receiver in its cradle, thinking about him, wishing he were in her arms right now, holding her as a man holds the woman he adores. His kisses, tender and sweet, all over her face, throat, cheeks, and then, her mouth. Finally, almost painstakingly, he would claim her lips and hold her in a mesmerizing dance of tongues. She sits at her desk, daydreaming about him until she feels the familiar throb of desire as it sweeps from her heart and settles like a slow heat, burning between her thighs. A flutter of pre-orgasmic pleasure bounces through her extremities, and she closes her legs a bit tighter, trying to prolong that exquisite feeling of pleasure. His sex and no one else's was the only thing that could satisfy her now. She craves his touch, the sensual movement of his fingers upon every inch of her body. Her body throbs and aches for him as she has never ached for anyone else before.

Had anyone dared to ask, she could not define their strange-or was it more accurately estranged—relationship. Why did this man have this effect on her? She doesn't really know. It just was. At times, late at night, she wanted to talk to him more than anything, more than anyone else, in the entire universe. But her fingers never quite make it to the telephone to punch in his number, to put the distance that had engulfed them aside. Normally, she was a very confident woman, but not when it came to Raheem. Even the sound of his name rolling off her tongue, like a secret, was a mystery to her, but in a sweet mystical type way. Who was he really? What did he want from life? What had he ever wanted from her?

She taps one long manicured nail lightly against her cheek and stares at the phone, wanting to call him back and put an end to this chasm that has somehow built itself around them, but fear holds her back. What if he really doesn't want her? No, that was a fact she couldn't bear to know for sure. The possibility that they could one day be together again kept her from losing her mind. Surely, she'd crack if she knew for certain that he no longer loved her, no longer wanted her, no longer craved her as she did him.

But in her heart she knows better. How else could one explain the frequent calls he made to her. The questions that he never asked seemed to silently hang in the air, like a ghost with no voice. His presence, or lack thereof, haunted her.

It was not so long ago that she made the difficult choice to ask him to give her more—more of himself, his time, his attention, his love. And that was the beginning of the end for them. She remembers how he refused her in a gracious sort of way, telling her that he could not give her what she wanted—not now anyway, he'd said. He also told her to do what she had to do, whatever she felt would make her happy. And with a tearing of her heart, she slunk away from him that day and hated herself for crying. Life goes on, people continue to live their lives from day to day. You find a way to move on. That was how she comforted herself for the remainder of that day and the many long ones that followed. But then, after a period of time, he would call, and all her resolve of moving on would crumble like a mound of dirt being blown away to the four corners of the earth. He'd call. She'd hold her breath and wait for him to simply say "I miss you. Come home, back to me. I love you."

It hadn't happened yet.

The telephone rings again, and her heart beats wildly in her chest. Could it be that she has summoned him? Can he hear— feel—her longing for him from miles away?

"Yes," she hears him say after she has said hello.

"Yes, what?"

"I miss you."

She smiles, actually grins like a Cheshire cat, so pleased to finally hear him say the words.

"Can I see you?" he asks.

"When?" she replies.

"Tonight."

"Yes," she says far too quickly. She hates herself for being so eager, but the answer rushes from her before she can even pretend to think about it.

With breathless anticipation she arrives later that evening to grace his doorstep. He opens the door, says hello, then walks away, leaving her to close the door herself. No hug, no kiss, nothing. She timidly follows him to the back of the house, to his bedroom. He is, as usual, engrossed in a televised basketball game—the playoffs, he tells her, as he scoots over to allow her to sit beside him. His eyes never leave the television. This is not what she had envisioned all day. In her daydreams, he would greet her with hot, urgent kisses, strip her of all her clothes, leaving her panties in a bunch upon the floor, her bra tossed casually aside. But reality rarely comes close to fantasy.

"Raheem, I thought you wanted me to come over so we could talk...not watch the game." She sighs, trying desperately not to sound like a disappointed child.

He gazes at her as if seeing her for the first time. He places a quick dry kiss on her lips and utters, "Just a few more minutes, babe."

She breathes a heavy sigh. "Mind if I take a quick shower?"

"Um-um," he mumbles.

"Do you still have the sponge and shower gel I left?"

"Um-hm."

She stares down at him long and hard and starts to wonder what she has ever seen in him. He is boring and selfish. Why did she come? What did she expect? She suddenly feels very tired, used, rejected. A shower will pick up her spirits, awaken her mind, and give her a chance to think. If he is still glued to the television set when she comes out, then she will put her clothes on and hit the door, she decides.

Once she has finally stripped, she examines her brown body in the mirror, for the most part liking what she sees, and what she does-n't like she has come to accept. Her belly seems to tell the story of her life: the babies she's had, her surgeries, faint scars from the car accident that nearly killed her. It's all there marring the skin that used to be brown, beautiful, and flawless. In her younger years her belly was firm and tight—you could bounce a coin off it—but those days were over, and she wonders if Raheem likes what he sees when he looks at her. Does he appreciate who she is?

She steps into the shower and the water hits her hard and strong. It is hotter than she usually likes it, but it feels good against her skin. The scent of strawberries awakens her senses, and the feel of the soft sponge against her wet, slippery body is heavenly. She lathers herself and washes several times before finally making the decision to leave the aquatic sanctuary. She wraps one of Raheem's thick towels around her ample breasts, noticing that it doesn't completely cover her. She wonders how Raheem will feel about the fact that she is letting her pubic hair grow back. He liked it shaved, and while they were together she kept it either completely bald or cut very close. It didn't seem to be a necessary part of her grooming anymore, now that they were apart.

A rush of steam, coupled with the strong scent of strawberries precede her as soon as she opens the bathroom door. Raheem has turned off the television, the sexy tones of a saxophone and the melodious flutter of a flute waft through the air, along with the fragrant aroma of incense—Black Love. She knows it well. It's their scent.

He sits on the edge of the bed, completely naked now, and watches her approach him, trying to hide herself under the towel. He wants to laugh because it is without much success and unnecessary, because in a few minutes the towel will be history. She is still modest, and she is still the most beautiful woman he's ever known. Though he's never told her that.

"What are you up to, naked buzzard?" she asks him playfully with a hint of sexiness.

He doesn't respond verbally. His smile tells her everything she needs to know. He grabs her around the waist and buries his face between her thighs. She hears him inhale deeply then exhale, his warm breath against her throbbing clit. Her liquid love begins to trickle down. She tries to keep the towel in place with one hand and cradle his head with the other, holding him right in the spot she wants him to be.

"You stopped shaving," he mumbled.

"Um-hm."

He tugs at the towel then, causing it to drop around her ankles. She throws back her head, opens her mouth, and moans. His tongue, hot and urgent, is leaving a wet trail on her clit. He urges her leg up to rest upon his shoulder. His fingers probe her, forcing her lips apart. He strokes her with his tongue, long strokes from anus to clit. His tongue darts in and out of her, and she can hear him moan. He utters murmurs of delight as if tasting her is the one thing in the world that gives him utmost pleasure.

He grabs her butt, applying gentle pressure, then releasing. He squeezes and releases her at the same time keeping rhythm with his ardent licks. His thumb enters her secret place, and the rhythm continues. She feels her vagina beginning to contract.

"Oh, my god...I'm cuming," she screams.

He knows she'll lose her balance and fall, so he quickly grabs her, and she collapses on the bed. He falls to his knees and continues to lap up all her juices, leaving her breathless and spent.

"No," she says, her voice a raspy whisper. "I want to feel you inside...cum inside."

He straddles her, his dick hard, the tip glistening with pre-cum, she notices. She grabs him and strokes him firmly. The overwhelming urge to taste him comes over her. With a suddenness that surprises him she sits up and claims him with her mouth. He tastes sweet. They begin to moan at the same time. Ecstasy has taken over. He begins to rock his hips back and forth, forcing himself in and out of her mouth as she gently holds his balls in her hand, stroking his sensitive spots.

"I'm gonna cum," he says between clenched teeth. Sweat trickles down his chest, off his forehead and into his eyes.

She releases him, lays back and plants her feet firmly on the bed, pushes herself up to meet him as he plunges deep inside her. She yelps. The feeling is bittersweet as she crosses the thin line between pleasure and pain. She rides that line right now and loves it. She bucks with as much force as he pushes. They rock and rock. He plunges deeper and deeper as she squeezes him with her inner muscles and takes all eight inches of him. They are each other's match tonight.

He finally allows himself to surrender, and surrender he does inside her walls.

As he lays beside her, panting as if he has run a marathon, she leaves delicate kisses on his chest, his ears, each nipple.

Then she whispers in his ear, "Did you miss me?"

He blinks several times, licks his lips and stares at her for a long time. Finally, when she is convinced he isn't going to answer her, he takes her in his arms, kisses her forehead and simply answers, "Yeah, sweetie, I missed you, and I love you."

In Search Of

I'm in search of some good dick. Not any old kinda dick. Good dick! Period. The kind that makes you holla with joy, helping you cross over the thin line of pain into pure unadulterated ecstasy. Yessssss. I don't want no pencil dick, short dick, my-hand-is-bigger-than-it kinda dick. I want good dick. The kind that is thick and long, stretch yo stuff wide, pound you into submission, reaching for that glorious high like touching the blue in the sky. Orgasm. Yeah, that's what I'm talking about.

I search faces in all kinds of places. Measure expertly with my eyes, the size of hands, thickness of fingers, length of feet. There is so much truth to what some perceive to be a lie. Hands and feet tell a lot. Oh, and recently I also heard a man's neck is also a clue. I ain't too sure about that one though, so I think I'll stick to checking out bulges, hands, feet, and firm thighs. And butt. Oh yes, got ta have a serious butt too. It's got to be round and smooth, make my clit jump just thinking about running my hand over the mocha-colored smooth skin, with fine hair—barely there—tickling my fingertips, making the palms of my hands sweat with anticipation of feeling that slick, thick dick inside of me.

Good dick. Yeah.

I don't care what nobody says. Especially them women who

claim they don't like sex, or they don't want to talk about sex, or snicker behind their hands when I speak of making love until the backs of your knees trickle sweat. Them kind of women get on my nerves. Yes, they do. You know why? Because they lie. Or they have fooled themselves into believing that only a man deserves to get sexual satisfaction. Forget that mess. God made man and woman. She wouldn't discriminate against our getting our freak on, now would She? Women need to just let go. Stop all that prissy mess and acting like they don't like being touched. Every woman likes to be touched, caressed, and then blessed with an ample dick stuck deep inside her. Every woman likes to at least try to get to the big O. Some women make all that damn noise like they see on triple-X movies or television. Don't they realize that a real man—a real lover—knows a real scream from a fake purr? If he is paying attention, is on his J-O-B, he does.

But I ain't really mad at them women who fake. They really ain't got much choice, do they? Too bad for them cause I ain't holding my tongue when the loving didn't come to me right. I have kicked many a man outta my bed who, at first glance, looked like he had it going on, just to find out after the lights were out, that he was sorely lacking in all areas of what I consider an expert at love. Like a man who wants to try and make me suck on his limp dick. I ain't doing that. No, sir! It's got to be hard and ready to receive my attentions, 'cause then I know without a doubt that he is ready to serve me, and that he is as turned on as I am. A man who can't get it up turns me off—well, that and bad breath. However, a man with halitosis can be dealt with. I simply turn my head and give few if any kisses, but there ain't much I can do with a member that isn't ready for me because my skills don't include making a man show desire. It has got to be a given for me. Because in bed I can only be described as phenomenal!

Now I am a professional woman, and there is nothing about me that would suggest that I am a straight-up freak, but I am. On the job I am all business, serious, and a take-charge kind of woman. I am the same in bed, but my coworkers do not need to know that. In my line of work, I travel a lot. I have become accustomed to outlandish one-night stands in cities all over the United States. Today I am heading to Atlanta. I only travel business class, which for me means, first class all the way, baby.

As I stand waiting impatiently for my United Airlines flight to pre-board, I notice a nice-looking black man decked out in a wool smoked— gray double-breasted suit. I know Armani when I see it. I am instantly intrigued but I can't seem to catch this brotha's eye. All his attention is fixed on his laptop. His cell phone rings, and I can hear his voice—deep and rich—talking in somewhat muted tones as if he doesn't really want anyone to overhear him. I watch him nod his head a time or two, as if the person he is talking to can see him; then he closes his laptop, glances around the terminal as he continues to nod and listen. Finally, his eyes land on me. I smile and dip my head slightly in a gesture of hello, to which he does the same. He continues to gaze at me while he holds his conversation and suddenly he laughs, a loud, hearty laugh. Someone has told him a good joke. With laughter and a smile still clinging to face, he concludes his call. He begins to shake his head as if in wonder about what he has just heard, and his laughter begins again.

"Attention, ladies and gentlemen, United Flight 525 with service to Atlanta will now begin pre-boarding. For those passengers with small children or the elderly who need extra time, you may board now. We will begin boarding our first-class passengers in one moment."

I slip my newspaper under my arm and gather my belongings— one carry-on, my Versace purse, and Coach briefcase. Our eyes briefly meet again as I notice him looking at me, his laptop already closed and ready to go. No luggage, I notice. As the boarding call begins for first-class passengers, I see him leave the area. What a disappointment, he isn't even on this flight. Oh, well, it really doesn't matter. I certainly can't get my flirt on with a man who might be seated in coach.

Seat 4A. Right before the coach seats began, only a flimsy curtain would separate me from the other passengers. Maybe he'd be seated in the bulkhead, he had long legs, I noticed, perhaps that is where he would request to be seated.

It's time for me to stop daydreaming and make a few calls before I am forced to put my cell phone away. I call my office and quickly become distracted by all my assistant has to tell me. Between making entries on my Palm Pilot, I glance out the window. I feel the weight of someone who has sat beside me. My eyes roll up into my head as I prayed this person is not a talker. I want to sleep on this flight. It isn't until I hear the instructions to turn off cell phones that I realize the plane is fully loaded and ready to take off. I flip my phone shut and dare to glance at my riding companion.

It's him.

I smile and utter an embarrassed hello.

"I noticed you in the terminal," he said.

I shake my head in agreement. "Yes. I saw you too. I thought you were on another flight."

"Oh, really. What made you think that?"

"You left," I say somewhat sarcastically.

"Had to get some gum. I have to chew gum or the air pressure is too much for me."

"Oh," I say and immediately began to think of babies and how bad they cry when we take off and land. Gets on my nerves. I chuckle and say, "You don't cry, do you?"

To my surprise, he laughs with me. "Nope. I don't cry. But if I did, would you comfort me?"

I snort a little and say, "I'm not the maternal type."

"Oh, so I take it you have no children?"

"None."

"Career woman?"

"Definitely."

"Is this trip business or pleasure?"

I steal a look at him, thinking he is a little bit nosy. "I was hoping it would be both."

"We could make the pleasure part of your trip start right here, right now."

"Really," I say. "How do you propose that?"

"It gets real quiet on these late-night flights. Everyone pretty much goes to sleep. But you and I could say awake and...talk?"

He says it with a questioning tone, and I immediately pick up on what he means.

"I was hoping to catch some sleep myself, but I could be persuaded to stay awake."

The flight attendant interrupts our playful banter by asking what we want to drink.

"Scotch rocks," he responds. "And the lady would like?" he asks me.

"The same. Thanks."

With drinks in hand, we relax, turn off the overhead light, lying in wait for the few people in first class to fall asleep.

"What is your name?" I ask him.

"Anthony."

"Jackie." We shake hands, his cold hand embraces mine; then he turns my hand over and kisses the palm, and before I realize it, he is licking the center of my hand in a slow, seductive circular motion.

"Oh...nice," I speak—moan, while the heat of his probing tongue continues to dance around the tender flesh of my palm. "Do you always tongue kiss stranger's hands?"

"Only strangers who are part of the club."

"The club?" I ask, suspiciously.

"Yes. The Above the Clouds Club. You have heard of it, haven't you?" he asks, teasing me with his eyes.

"What do members of this club do?" I ask, teasing him as well.

"They join hips above the clouds, when the lights are out and all is silent except for the hiss and moan of the strange lovers' breathing."

"You know, Anthony, you could be wrong about me being a member of this club. You might have completely insulted me."

A twinkle in his eyes appears. "Did I insult you?"

"Grab a blanket and a couple of pillows. I think I'm going to catch some shut eye."

He smirks at me, then stands to gather what I have asked for. I notice the bulge in his pants once he turns to the side. Yep, he is ready for me.

Once we are securely snuggled beneath the rough, cheap, navy blue blankets, I manage to wriggle out of my Victoria Secret panties, and hold them in a ball in my fist. He takes them from me, inhales deeply, and sighs. With great care and agility I straddle his lap. His dick is already out, standing straight up, waiting to impale me. I don't ease myself on to him. No, not yet. Instead I hold him in my hands so I can measure his length and girth. Nice. And more than adequate. The smell of his cologne and his own body scent send waves of desire coursing swiftly through me. I stroke him for a little while, then with my hand outstretched, hold him at attention as I gyrate my clit against his shaft. I press the hot center of me harder and harder against his dick for maximum pressure to induce an orgasm for me. I lift myself up, as if ready to let him inside of me; then I just slide down the side of him, driving him crazy with my wetness. I can hear his breathing, hot and rapid, against my ear.

"You're driving me crazy," he says.

I only hum my pleasure in his ear and continue to stroke myself with his dick, mixing my juices with his. It isn't long before everything is slick and fragrant, the smell of our musk strong under the blanket.

"Put your finger inside me," I demand.

He does as I request. I know I am about to explode so I lift myself up again, and his finger leaves the inside of me with an audible pop. Then I ease down on him, slow and deliberate, still holding his shaft with my hand. His mouth goes slack, and he utters a soft moan as I begin to squeeze then release him within my vaginal walls.

He slides farther down in the chair. He seems to be anchoring himself; then with force that almost knocks me over, he begins to pound me with strong, powerful strokes, his hips rocking as his dick slams into me like he is trying to enter my throat from this vantage point. I meet him thrust for thrust, my power matching his. I can feel the leather of the first-class seats beginning to irritate my knees, but I don't care. He wants to play like this, oh, I'm all for it. It's on.

We have to be careful not to be too noisy. The last thing we need

is an interruption that might make us stop our privately public interlude. I try to keep my panting to a minimum, but sweat has started to
trickle down my face, and I am suddenly very thirsty, and homeboy
looks like he will be at it for a while. Good, I think, I like a man with
stamina.

He nibbles on my neck, and then he whispers in my ear, "You like
that dick, girl, huh. You like this big fat dick inside of you."

"It's all right," I reply, smile and kiss his lips as if to say "shut up
and keep it coming."

His erogenous zone must have been his lips because as soon as
I make contact with him—my full lips against his—he begins to moan
louder, his lips gliding against mine, his tongue swirling and dipping
and diving. All the while he purrs like a cat. It doesn't take long
before I notice that his thrusting has gotten a little less aggressive,
and his tongue has stopped dancing.

"I'm going to cum," he says in a whisper. "Inside or out."

I don't respond audibly, just yank myself from him and let his
semen squirt all over him. It's cruel, but hey I don't care.

As he disgustedly begins to clean himself up, I pull my panties
back on, and immediately ring the overhead bell for the flight attendant.

When she appears I say, "Two more scotches, please. We're
both very thirsty."

He looks at me, and I at him, and we both begin to laugh out loud
as if that's the best joke ever told.

In Between the Night

by

Angelique

Chapter One

*T*he summer sun is shimmying lower, leaving that filmy, almost grainy feel to the world. That halfway point between light and dark when it's hard to tell between good and bad, right and wrong. People shed their loose-flowing day selves like soiled panties and strap on the tight fit of darkness, which can hide as well as seek.

One by one the cat-eyed streetlights pop on over my head, the switch hit with the click of my heels against the hard, gray concrete of New York City streets—at night. Yesss. Twilight. Perfect time. My time. Slipping into darkness.

The hint of blackness slides along my veins, pumping, electrifying, setting my juices flowing. Wet, now, between my thighs. I feel the tingle like a silky tongue running along my spine.

Twilight. My time.

By day they call me Margaret, the quiet, bespeckled secretary who eats bologna sandwiches brought from home-alone at her desk. Margaret doesn't have many friends, doesn't have much of a life. Or so it seems. And I like it like that. They need never know. Only Anthony knows the truth. Every Wednesday. But it is Jade who controls the night with a sway of her hips, moving to a slow bluesy rhythm. The jut and jiggle of her breasts barely contained in the nearly sheer blouse that tempts all who can almost see the hard, purple nipples beneath. Close enough to touch, but not quite, not yet.

I am Jade. I am twilight-slipping into darkness.

Hot flesh brushes by me, bumping, rubbing in the push and tug of the busy streets. The street dwellers want to feel me, touch me, smell me. They are drawn to me like an exploring tongue hungry to stroke the pearly pink clit that swells with need. Soon.

Yes, twilight, when nothing is as it seems.

The music inside and out draws me to it, matching my beat. Yes, this is the place—for tonight.

I push through the glass doors, stepping into the cool confines of hot red lights and cool blues, dark enough to hide, bright enough to be seen. The murmurs are low, one long, lazy river stream of sound, playing beneath the bass and black and white ivories. I smile and slowly scan the tight spaces, filled with heads bowed close together, lips almost touching, hands hidden beneath tables to stroke a naked leg, caress the growing cocks that throb between hard, muscled thighs.

"Haven't seen you here before."

The voice is hot at my neck, stirring the tiny hairs. My cat opens and closes. I turn, slowly. Needy breasts brush against his chest— nipples meeting nipples in a teasing dance of introduction.

"Now that you've found me ..." I let the words linger.

Bodies move around us, pressing us closer. Cloaked in the semi-darkness. Twilight. His cock trapped now between my trained thighs. His eyes squeeze shut as my grip tightens, the bodies pressing us closer, the music swaying. We move together in a perfect note.

Nimble fingers cut through the thin space of air that separates us. Eye to eye. Cat to cock. I smile, taking him in my hand, taunting fingertips tease the head, milking out his juice which drips along the curve of my palm. I bring it to my mouth and lick the spicy drink, as thick fingers slip inside me.

He shudders to realize that nothing stands between him and the entrance to my cat, which grins in wet welcome. Thighs spread. Inviting. Waiting. He dips down, then straight up, cupping my butt— as if I wanted to get away—pushing the hard knot of his cock deep within the pulsing walls that grip and release letting the white river flow.

Our cries and groans are muffled by the rhythm of the band, the slap and grind of our hips hidden by the bodies that swirl around us, pressing us closer-faster, slower. Moving to the beat.

Bent head, almost in prayer, seeks solace between the hot swell of my breasts, finding absolution on a tingling purple nipple that grows between teeth and tongue.

No words are spoken, needed. The understanding that this dark, secret moment, this coupling is all we want. For now.

Hard fingers dig into my butt, clamping me tighter, pulling me faster. I want it. More. Deeper. Longer. Don't let the music end.

Waves radiate deep down in my belly, spread along the length of my thighs and back up to pool in my cat, which opens and closes. Faster. Harder. Don't let the music end—as the room moves away-disappears into the twilight. Just us. Coming. On the dance floor, bumping, grinding to the music.

A long, deep thrust. A swelling, a trembling that fills me, spreads me, releases me. Our cries mix with the music, play tenor to the bass, wiggles between the black and white keys and smooths out on a long, soulful note.

Yes, twilight hides as well as seeks. The darkness slides through my veins. Electrifies.

My cat smiles wide, releasing his thickness from inside me. His cum trickles down my thighs—sticky and wet. He releases the purple nipple—his penance complete.

The bodies swallow me whole, urge me toward the glass doors and out into what is now the blackness of night. My heels click against the gray concrete. The wetness between my thighs, squishing, dripping as I strut beneath the cat-eyed lights.

"Wait!"

I smile, the scent of our sex filling my head, making me dizzy with wanting—more.

"Wait!"

I knew he would come—come after me. Ask my name.

A yellow cab grinds to a halt at the curb. I look behind me once. Memorize his face, slip into the cab and speed away.

"Jade," I whisper and smile, dipping my finger into the cum that clings to my pussy cat, bringing it to my mouth—to remember—twilight and the slow drag beneath the hot red and cool blue lights.

I lean back and close my eyes, dipping my finger in and out, harder and faster. I know he's watching me, can't help himself. I spread my legs wider. Don't want him to have an accident straining to see what treasures are hidden within my wet, pink hole.

I wasn't always this way—on the prowl, seeking satisfaction, heels clicking against the gray concrete. It's really Anthony's fault. He thought he was helping me. Helping me not to be Margaret, but Jade.

And now he wants to control me, control it—this thing that consumes me, consumes us. But it's loose now, released—unstoppable.

I raise my leg. Press my heel against the back of the front seat. Deeper. Two fingers. Three.

I open a button. Right breast bursts free, teased by the breeze that blows through the open window.

The cab bounces and bumps. In and out. Three fingers go deeper, wetter, wider. My body shudders. The driver moans. I know he has his cock out now, stroking it up and down with his free hand, trying to watch me, watch the road. I scream out in pleasure as the climax shoots through me, leaving me weak, slumped against the ratty leather seat—just as his jism splashes against the windshield. I laugh and step out of the cab—my payment made.

I never wanted to tell anyone about my other self, my Jade self, my hidden self. No one would believe me—quiet Margaret. No one except Anthony. It was Anthony who helped me find Jade—release her from the confines of my puritanical upbringing.

Actually, I met Anthony quite by accident. As usual I was having lunch alone. But on this particular day, instead of sitting at my desk decided to take my bologna sandwich to the park.

The day was warm for spring. Already I could feel my skin tingle beneath the rays of the sun, heat from the outside in—warming me all over. I almost smiled, knowing what true heat was like—from the inside out. But I held on to my secret while taking tiny bites of my sandwich, watching clandestine couples pretend not to be lovers. I knew all about pretense.

I was taking a sip of my diet iced tea when a long shadow fell over me, blocking out the sunlight. I shielded my eyes with a cupped palm and looked up.

"Why are you eating alone?" the smooth deep voice asked.

I squinted against the sun, trying to make out the figure above me. *Long, dark, lean* were the words to describe him that immediately came to my mind.

"Perhaps I'm waiting for someone," I answered and tried to look away but I couldn't. It was as if my eyes had become glued to the ones that held mine. I saw him smile.

"If you are, you've been waiting a long time."

"You've been watching me."

"I hope you don't mind," he said, moving closer, bringing his own heat.

I tore my gaze away and tried to concentrate on my sandwich and not the heaviness that rested comfortably between his thighs. "Are you alone, too?" I asked, almost afraid of the answer, but needing it to be yes.

"I was." He eased down beside me on the grass, pulled up several blades and twisted them between his fingers. "But not anymore." He turned to me, ran his tongue lightly over his lips, and his eyes crinkled in the corners as if he'd just told a joke. "What's your name?"

I swallowed. Men never asked me my name, not my Margaret name. No one had ever been interested in that persona. Nervously I brushed at my hair with my hand. He took my hand, held it, ran his thumb across my knuckles.

"Margaret," I answered in a voice I barely recognized. It was low, husky almost. It thrilled my ears, and I wondered if it thrilled him as well.

He continued to lightly rub his thumb across my knuckles, then along my fingers. "Hmmm." He tilted his head to the side, looked at me curiously. "You don't look like a Margaret to me." He pursed his lips in thought. "More like a ... Jade. Yes, Jade. That's what I'll call you. Do you like that name?"

I nodded numbly. "Y-ess."

He released my hand and reached for my cheek, then removed my glasses and set them on the grass beside us. "Your eyes are too beautiful to hide behind those." He stroked my brow, which brought a reluctant smile to my face.

I lowered my gaze. I could feel the warmth building in my belly. He was so close. Close enough to touch. I wanted to.

He took my hand and placed it against his heart. It was racing, like horses charging toward the finish line. A hot, sticky flow seeped from between the deep center of me, wetting my panties. I tightened my thighs.

"I'd like to see you again, Jade. Would you like that?"

I nodded, afraid to speak, afraid of that new voice again.

He reached into the inside pocket of his navy blue suit jacket and pulled out a card, then handed it to me. *Anthony Tate, Psychiatrist.* Psychiatrist! I wasn't crazy. Was that what he thought...because I ate alone in the park...that I was crazy?

"I can make you, Jade, make you feel like the real woman you are inside...the one dying to get out." He smiled, almost tenderly, I thought.

My gaze snapped up, battled with his. "Who-who is this Jade? Who do you think she...I am?"

"Come and see me on Wednesday, and we will begin to find her...together." He rose, looked down at me. "I'll be waiting." He turned and walked away, merged with the crowd and was gone.

I returned to work, settled down at my desk, answered the phones, typed the letters and responded to all the mundane requests made of a secretary. But my mind was on the man in the park. *Anthony Jade...Anthony.* What did he know? What could he see?

Did he smell the heat that always lingered around me? Did he sense my secret desires, yet unfulfilled? Did he know of the passions that simmered inside me? Would I become this...this Jade, this other woman who I, too, believed lurked in my soul?

Questions, questions, they haunted me, taunted me, followed me home, filled my head and my dreams. Restless with something unnamed, I tossed and turned all night, eager for morning, eager for Wednesday...for Anthony. What would we find...together?

My legs felt weak as I stood in front of the elevator waiting for the doors to open. His offices were on the fifteenth floor. My heart jumped once then settled as the doors slid open. I drew in a long breath and stepped inside the metal container. Wednesday.

The doors opened on my floor. I froze.

"Getting off?" the old black elevator operator asked.

How long had he been doing this job, I suddenly wondered. How many faceless faces had he seen? What whispered conversations had he overheard while pretending to study the lighted dials...1, 2, 3.

"Miss...?" This time he sounded annoyed, as if I were holding up his day, delaying him from arriving at some important destination. The sixteenth floor, I thought wickedly, and almost laughed.

I brushed by him and could sense him watching me, shaking his head sadly at what he thought was my confusion. I wasn't confused. I was on the hunt...seeking Jade.

I pulled the card from my purse and checked the office number—1527. I headed left, down the silent, carpeted corridor with its white doors and gold letters. 1523, 1525...1527. I stood there for a moment, suddenly unsure. Is this what I really wanted?

Yes, that voice whispered in my ear.

I knocked. There was no answer. I tried again. Silence. I checked the number against the card. Today was Wednesday. This was 1527. So what was wrong? I reached for the knob and turned. The door opened silently.

Angelique

It took a moment for my eyes to adjust to the dimness. There was a simple desk, a long brown leather couch and several chairs. All empty. Plants stood in huge pewter pots and soft music came from some hidden place. A standing rack of magazines graced one corner of the rectangular room, and a bookcase of assorted novels, biographies and psychological studies took up one wall. A portable television was mounted on another. Just beyond the classy setup, a door to an adjoining room was partially ajar. I moved cautiously toward it, hesitated for two beats and then pushed it open just a bit more.

Anthony faced me, seated in a high-backed black leather chair, sipping a drink as if he were waiting for a date, instead of a client. He seemed totally calm.

"I was hoping you hadn't changed your mind. Come in." He placed the drink on the desk.

I did as he asked and closed the door behind me. It was even dimmer in this room—almost night. I moved to the far side of the room and took a seat on an overstuffed chair. It nearly wrapped around me, like a comforting cocoon, and I felt inexplicably safe. I laid my purse on my lap.

"How have you been?"

"Fine."

"Why don't we start by having you take off . . . your glasses."

I swallowed hard, slipped off my glasses and put them in my purse.

Anthony stood and moved from behind his desk toward me. My pulse beat madly in my throat. He took my hand gently and pulled me to my feet.

"I think I have something that will fit you perfectly." He moved away into the next room and returned shortly with a tiny piece of black cloth in his hands. "Why don't you put this on and then we can begin."

What was going on? What had I gotten myself into? First the glasses and now this. What kind of psychiatrist was he?

"I can see the questions dancing in your eyes." He stepped closer, and I inhaled the intoxicating scent of him. A seductive, masculine fragrance of musk. I turned my back to him, afraid of what I saw reflected in his eyes—me, wanting him. "I have a very unique way of dealing with those who come to me," he continued. "I sense what they need, and I give it to them." He paused, and I felt his smile brush across my neck.

What I should have done was run straight out of the door. But I didn't. My curiosity about him and his methods was too overpowering, too great. I had to know more about this man.

In the tranquil darkness of the room, I felt my suspicion melt slowly as his voice took on a soothing, almost paternal tone. Anthony stood behind me, both of his hands resting on my shoulders, letting some time lapse before holding out the black dress. He lowered his head behind me, his lips close to my ear. "Just relax. You'll see. Everything will be fine. Now...go and change. I'll wait right here." His words seemed to enter my flesh, like short bursts of electricity, urging me to trust him, to place myself completely under his spell. "We only have an hour," he whispered.

In the next room I held the tiny bit of black cloth in my hand. One by one I unfastened the buttons of my brown dress, released the matching fabric belt and stepped out of the calf-length outfit—a suitable, respectable dress. A plain white bra and cotton panties adequately covered any hint of forbidden flesh that constantly burned beneath. I removed my bra, and my breasts seemed to sigh in relief from the loosening of their constraints. I took one look behind me to the closed door, a moment of indecision, then back at the mirror before slipping the dress over my head.

It slid across my body like tender fingertips, like lightly caressing silk, in search of soft flesh, arousing the sensitive nerves. Briefly, my eyes shut as a sudden tremor fluttered through me. When I opened my eyes, disbelief was painted on my face. This person, this woman reflected in the mirror was not me, not Margaret. It couldn't be. This was someone else, a lustful female ready to take pleasure wherever she could find it. *He knew.* He knew the liberating effect the dress would produce, freeing me of all false morality, of all inhibitions. The short, clingy black dress with its thin straps and flounce skirt that didn't come anywhere in the vicinity of my knees, made me look...daring, sultry, totally feminine and wanton. Everything that I'd always felt inside, but had been too afraid to tap, was there before me. In the mirror, I was sex. I was desire. Now here she stood, facing me, daring me to step out into the other room, begin the process of finding Jade. How did he know? How could...

"You look just as I thought you would." His laugh held a bit of mischief.

I covered my breasts, knowing that my hardened nipples were clearly defined against the fabric, clearly announcing my arousal, my awakening.

Anthony moved closer, closer. He reached for my hands and gently brought them to my sides. I didn't resist him. I submitted willingly, even as he slowly unfastened the barrette that held my ponytail in place. He turned me back toward the mirror. His breath was hot on my neck, then teasing like a frisky tongue in my ear.

"Look," he urged. "Look at her." His hands cupped my shoulders. I could feel the heat of his fingers sear my flesh. "Look at the gorgeous woman you've been hiding. Embrace her, accept her, feel her." His hands slid down my arms, then raised them above my head, lifting the dress even higher in the process. A hint of my white panties peeked out from beneath the hem. Suddenly I felt like removing them as well, the last of my inhibitions—release the scent of my womanhood. *Not now, not yet,* my conscience cautioned.

"Remember this woman you see before you, remember how you feel at this very moment when you leave here and go back into the world," he said in a low voice. "This is the woman you've been seeking. This is your sensual self, your sexual self. She is strong, powerful, totally female. She will not need to seek permission for anything she does. You will never look at your femininity again in the same way. I guarantee you that. This is the real you. This is Jade."

He sounded so sure, so certain of what he was saying, what he was making me believe. As I stared at my reflection, I felt my hidden power, I longed for the sensual feline that prowled beneath. My eyes sought his in the mirror. They were dark, hungry. My nipples stood erect, the heaviness of my breasts seeming to fill all the more, taunted by the erotic brushing of the fabric against my bare flesh.

The music drifted around us, cool as an April breeze. I closed my eyes and leaned against him, as if I belonged there, right there. His arms slid around my waist, pulling me closer, possessing me. We swayed to the music as one body, linked, synchronized.

"You must release her, release Jade," Anthony whispered into my hair. "All you've ever wanted, ever needed is there for the taking. Believe that. Tell me you believe it, Jade."

"I-I believe," I stuttered, a riot of sensation rocketing through me in waves. His hands stroked my hips in time with the music. A pulse beat between my thighs, and I was thankful that I'd kept on my panties to absorb the dew that dripped and pooled there.

"Jade will be our secret," he said." Yours and mine."

"Yes," I uttered, helpless under the hypnotic cadence of his voice. The room grew warmer, closer.

"Only in between the night. Those moments before darkness pushes the light away. That is Jade's time."

I turned toward him, looked into his eyes, searching for understanding. "In between the night?"

"By day you are Margaret. By twilight you are Jade."

I gazed around me, felt the secure blanket of the semidarkness, the feel of the soft fabric against my flesh, the tingle of my nipples, the dampness between my thighs, the yearning for something that was now within my reach. And I understood.

"You must promise me one thing," Anthony said.

"What is it?"

"You must only share the experiences of your new self with me. Tell me of your awakenings, your adventures. Will you promise me that?"

"Yes. I will tell only you."

He leaned down and tenderly brushed my forehead with a kiss. "Go now. Until Wednesday."

When I awoke the following morning, I was filled with a new energy. Even my standard white undies had a new feel against my flesh. I remembered everything that Anthony said, and I began to tingle all over.

I opened my closet door, and there was the dress. My juices flowed over my lips. How could a simple dress evoke such sensations? I wondered, suddenly thinking of all manner of voodoo and mojo. I laughed at my own foolishness, brushing the dress with my hand. It was just a dress after all. I reached for my army-green jacket and mid-calf skirt and prepared to get ready for work. I took one last look at the slinky black dress, smiled and closed my closet door.

As usual, at work, the staff basically ignored me, only speaking to me if they needed something. And that was fine. I had no need for conversation. I had a secret.

"You've been smiling to yourself all day, Margaret," Lynn, one of the other secretaries, commented. "What's going on in that head of yours? Finally found someone special?"

I ducked my head. I didn't want her to see what lurked behind my smile, in my eyes. I focused my attention on the letter I had to finish for my boss, Mr. Johnson.

"Nothing," I mumbled, and hoped that the sound of the keys and the rustling of paper would drown out the beating of my heart. Lynn was one of the few people at the law firm who'd tried to befriend me. She'd even asked me to join her for lunch a few times, or to hang out after work. I always declined. I wasn't really sure why, I just did. I always figured she simply felt sorry for me. And I didn't need or want anyone's sympathy.

"Well, it's nice to see you smile," she said, not at all turned off by my one-word answer. "You know you have a lovely smile, Margaret.

You should use it more often."

My eyes darted in her direction. It wasn't so much what she said, but how she said it. Not as a compliment, but some sort of invitation. She ran her tongue across her lips, held my astonished look for a moment longer and walked away.

I watched her, and suddenly felt heated. Her hips moved in a slow back-and-forth rhythm, her butt taking up just the right amount of space in her fitted lemon-yellow skirt. I couldn't seem to take my eyes off her. I tried to memorize her sultry walk, and wondered what it would feel like to get the kind of responses from men that she did as she passed them at their desks. I got up and followed her to the ladies' room.

Lynn turned from the mirror when I stepped in. Her mouth was a glossy red from a recent coat of lipstick. She smiled.

"Taking a little break?" she asked.

"Yeah. I...needed to get away for a minute."

She looked at me curiously for a moment. "I think this lipstick would look great on you, with your complexion." She held the tube out to me. "Try some."

"No...I don't"

"Aw, come on, just try some."

Tentatively, I reached for the tube. It almost seemed to beckon me.

"Try a little at first and see how you like it," Lynn encouraged.

I turned toward the mirror and with shaky fingers applied a light coat. It was almost like tasting Lynn, I thought, as the smooth cream slid over my lips. I licked them, committing the flavor to memory.

"Red is definitely your color," Lynn enthused, and I had to agree.

"Thanks," I mumbled shyly and handed the tube back to her.

"No, keep it. I can get more."

"Really?"

"No problem. Well, I better get back to work." She headed for the door, then stopped and turned back toward me. She put her right hand on her hip. "There's definitely something different about you today, Margaret. Definitely something different." She opened the door and walked out.

I turned toward the mirror, examined my reflection, saw myself in the slinky black dress with my red lips and lush nakedness beneath. Yes, there was something different about me today. It was Jade, dying to get out.

That evening, just before the sun set, I put on the black dress and the red lipstick and went out into the night. I needed to see how it felt, if strangers would see me differently, see what lurked beneath.

I took a slow stroll down the busy avenue, filled with after-work pedestrians, trying to find refuge from their day. I tried to imitate Lynn's walk with each step, letting myself become one with the dress, with the red lips, with the image. I felt alive as if electric currents were coursing through my body. The nylon stockings made a *swish-swish* sound in time to the *click-click* of my heels.

I wanted to laugh, to shout out to whoever would listen just how marvelous I felt. Yet, at the same time I was terrified. I felt as if I were on an unstoppable train, hurtling through a darkened tunnel with no idea what was on the other side.

Suddenly cautious, I gazed around me, took in the sights, inhaled the scents. There were men and women in all sizes and shapes, all colors, all modes of dress. There were couples, singles, mixed doubles. I walked among them hoping to find someone like me, someone searching, someone hidden beneath the exteriors.

As I passed by a tiny women's boutique, I stopped short. An overwhelming sense of something familiar began to fill me. There was a young woman inside that I could just make out from my side of the glass. She was tall-taller than me, gangly to some people. She wore black, heavy-rimmed glasses that made her brown eyes and small mousy face almost comical. Her wiry hair was plaited in a single braid that just cleared her shoulders. Thick-soled shoes, the kind you often see on old, broken-down women, covered her long, narrow feet. The simple blue dress she wore was just that, simple, not enough detail to describe.

She looked so lonely, so out of place in the trendy shop as she one by one went through the rack of flamboyant outfits in brilliant colors and incredible fabrics and styles. I stepped closer, drawn by her aloneness.

Suddenly it was if she sensed my presence; she looked straight at me, through those thick specs, through the plate-glass window, straight into my soul. My body visibly rocked as if I'd been shoved. But I didn't move. I couldn't.

A slow smile crept across her wide mouth, and her eyes darkened behind the lenses. She pulled a fire-engine red dress from the rack and held it up in front of her, her eyes glued to mine as if seeking my approval.

It was no more than a handkerchief held up against the length of the long, lanky body. And it seemed perfect. Exactly what she should have. The tiny chiffon dress, cinched at the waist was entirely see-through except for the strips of satin that would cover the breasts, crotch and butt.

Where could you go in a dress like that? I wanted to know. Where did she plan to go?

I stood there outside the shop as if glued to the spot. I watched the woman pay for the dress, then disappear into a room in the back. The sun was beginning to dip behind the horizon. A dull cast began to fall over the city, making it hard to distinguish images, maybe even thoughts. In between the night. I shivered, began to turn away when a flash of red caught my eye.

My heart pounded. Could this possibly be the same unattractive woman transformed into an alluring, provocative, sensual being? Her legs were the first thing that drew you, long, toned, a perfect brown encased in sheer stockings with a hint of sparkle; the tiny waist, breasts that demanded to be set free; perfect shoulders that set off the wild mane of hair giving the impression she'd just been thoroughly screwed. Gone now were the glasses, making way for the startling effect of her penetrating brown eyes, haloed by dark curling lashes and arching brows.

Angelique

The red dress fell across her curves like waves lapping against the shore, touching, teasing and leaving its mark—again and again.

She didn't walk out, she strutted. Head held high, almost tossed back in challenge, a wicked smile on her wet, red lips. She went right by me. I smelled her. Not her perfume—her. Her woman scent. That undetectable scent of a woman that men sniff after and women want to keep away from their men. I knew it. I smelled it around me in the privacy of my room. I smelled it with Anthony. A heat that seeps from your pores, spills out your woman need, surrounds you like an aura. Yes, I knew the scent, and I understood what she needed, what she sought. I was not alone. I would call her Amber.

I kept my distance but I didn't let her out of my sight. I needed to know where she was going. If I, too, could find refuge, satisfaction.

I followed her for about three blocks, watching in awe at the reactions of nearly everyone she passed. Men practically bumping into one another as they stared after her, women who shook their hips a bit faster, a bit wider to show they had what it took as well. Old men and women, who for a moment saw their younger selves, but gave in to whom they were now and simply shook their heads in disgust.

She didn't seem to notice or care. She was in her world, her space, dismissing everything around her except her destination. She swung her black laminated shopping bag lightly in her hand, made a sharp right turn down West Fourth Street and walked into a dimly lit bar/restaurant.

Timidly I stood outside, debating what to do next. Should I go in? Why not, I decided and entered. It took a moment for my eyes to adjust, and when they did, I spotted Amber instantly. She was seated at the bar, already in animated conversation, shifting her attention between the bartender and the man on her left and the one on her right.

I eased to the back unnoticed and took a seat at a vacant table, my line of sight perfect to watch Amber's performance. I committed to memory the way she stared into the eyes of the men when they spoke, blocking out everything else; the way she ran her tongue across her lips, tossed her head back in laughter, exposing the long line of her neck. The way she crossed her incredible legs, forcing the hem of the dress to inch up around her hips.

Her body, her mouth, her essence was in constant motion. You couldn't help but notice her, want to know more about her—be her.

A waitress came to my table, blocking my view.

"Something from the bar?"

I looked up. "A ginger ale, please."

She gave me a pitiful look and sauntered away.

When I looked back at the bar, Amber was gone. I scanned the darkness. It was as if she'd been an apparition. There was no sign of her. One of the two men was gone as well. I smiled to myself, imagining his joy at the hidden treasures Amber would share with him—bold enough to share with him—somewhere in the big city.

The waitress returned with my ginger ale. I sipped it slowly, contemplating all I'd seen and what I would do with what I'd witnessed. I paid for my drink, left a small tip and headed home. I could feel my insides smile as I meandered back toward my nondescript apartment. There was so much I needed to learn, to experience.

What satisfied me most about that night was the discovery that I was not alone. There was at least one other like me—maybe more. But for now there was Amber. I would see her again. I was sure of it.

During my next weekly visit to Anthony's office I told him about Amber and what I'd seen, how I felt a kinship, a sisterhood with the woman.

Anthony simply made some notes on a pad, nodded his head and reminded me to tell him everything.

"Don't leave anything out, Margaret, " he said in his shrink's voice of authority. My Father Confessor. "The only way our sessions together will work is if you are completely open and honest with me. Trust me. You do trust me don't you…Jade?"

"Yes, I trust you."

"Tell me more, Jade," Anthony insisted, locking his eyes on mine.

"Where should I begin?"

"At the beginning. The first time. Try to go back and tell me what made you Margaret."

"The beginning?" I repeated. I paused for a moment trying to recall the turning point for me, the moment when I knew I was different, that I was not the girl my parents sent off to Catholic school every day. "I was thirteen..."

Chapter Two

In trying to help you understand who I am, why I am, I need to go back to the early days, when innocence still lingered in my soul.

My mother and father were only lucky enough to have me. I found out many years later that they'd tried and failed. As a result they devoted all their time and energy to me, into making me the perfect daughter. Unfortunately, my mother and father were from another time, another brand of thinking. They were raised by very strict parents from the Caribbean who believed that children should be seen and not heard; that short skirts, makeup, dating, going to clubs and not attending Sunday Mass was tantamount to eternal damnation.

My parents, rather than embrace the moment, lived in the past and kept me there right along with them. My father's greatest fear was that some "unworthy" boy would find me attractive, find something of interest in me and ultimately lead me down the road of no return. The sex road. "Sex is something you must stay away from, Margaret," my father would caution in a deep, ominous voice. "All these young boys want is to get what you have. I don't want anything or anybody to ruin my baby girl."

Ruin.

"You keep those boys away from you, Margaret," my mother

would whisper before she'd kissed me good night. "Don't let them get near your private parts. And you don't touch them either. You stay a good girl. Understand?"

I would nod numbly, having grown used to the nightly warning and the awful things that one little slipup would cause.

I grew to fear this thing called sex, this thing that would forever change who I was, what I was. I was afraid of what it could do to me, some terrible thing from which I could never recover. I wanted to stay as far away from it as possible. I wanted to make my parents love me, believe in me. I wanted to remain a good girl. And I did—for a time.

For as long as I can remember I wore glasses. I wasn't even sure if I really needed them. They were just a part of my life. Thick-framed, black-rimmed glasses. A certain deterrent. My skirts were always below my knees, and jewelry was out of the question. I used to look at myself in the bathroom mirror, study my face. I wasn't bad to look at. My complexion is smooth, a soft brown. I had dark brown eyes that are turned up a bit at the ends. My lashes are long and my brows kind of silky and sweeping. My hair isn't what would be called "good hair" but I had plenty of it. However, I never got to show it off much because I always wore it in a ponytail. I was pretty tall and rather skinny. No real curves of which to speak. I think my mouth is my most interesting asset. It's wide and full, and my top lip has this great little dip in it, like a bow. But all of me was camouflaged in drab-ness.

I became accustomed to kids teasing me in school and took it in stride, even though I secretly envied their hip clothes and longed for the camaraderie of my female classmates and just one look of inter-est from a boy. Those things, however, were not to be. So, I learned to accept my fate, and for the first eight years of school I perfected the art of being invisible. My schoolbooks became my friends. I excelled in all of my classes. By the time I reached the eighth grade I'd been on the honor roll for three years running. My classmates began to notice that I knew everything and started seeking me out at lunchtime, and after school, wanting to know if I could help them study.

A part of me knew the reason for the interest was because I had something to offer, something to benefit them. It wasn't really me they cared about at all. But that was okay. I drank up the attention like someone lost in the desert and suddenly stumbling upon an oasis. I had friends now. I was a part of something. And even if it was only pretense, it felt good.

My parents didn't seem to mind that I was beginning to receive phone calls from classmates or that I brought a friend home from school—always a girl, of course—to study between bites of cookies and gulps of milk. That is, until my body began to betray me.

I'd just gotten out of the shower and was reaching for my towel hanging on the rack, when my mother stepped into the bathroom. Her eyes widened to twice their size when she saw me. There I was in my birthday suit, dripping wet, smelling like a burst of spring and feeling suddenly dirty.

"Margaret," she said in such a strange voice, I barely recognized it, and from the appalled look in her eyes, I knew there must be something wrong with me, wrong with my body. She grabbed the nearest towel, tossed it at me and practically ran out the door.

I didn't know what to make of my mother's bizarre behavior. At the tender age of thirteen all I could imagine was that there must be something terribly wrong with me and whatever it was, it upset my mother so badly that words couldn't express her anguish.

I turned to the mirror, trying desperately to see what hovered in her eyes. I rarely looked at myself—really looked—especially at my body. But I needed to know. Yet all I could see was warm brown skin that felt soft to the touch, a fullness where my once flat chest had turned to actual breasts, the nipples dark and hard. My straight up-and-down figure curved gently at the waist and a thick patch of curly hair now hid my other lips before flaring out to round hips and long legs.

I was afraid of this person in the mirror, this person I didn't recognize. And it frightened my mother, too. Tears rolled down my eyes. I didn't know what to do, how I could turn myself back into the person my mother could look at with love and not alarm.

Confused and ashamed, I dried myself off, careful not to linger too long at those untouchable places, and wrapped my robe tightly around me before tiptoeing to my bed.

My mother and I never spoke of that evening in the bathroom, but the parental warnings grew more intense. I began to wear layers of clothes to hide this new self I'd become what seemed like overnight and disappeared deeper into my shell, shunning the few pretend friends I'd made, afraid that they would discover my ugly secret.

Because of my grades I was accepted into all the top public high schools in New York. My parents, however, had no intention of giving me that much freedom, exposing me to the ugly world. They wanted me to remain sheltered and protected as long as the law and their last breaths would allow.

So, when I started high school that sunny September, it was at an all-girls Catholic school, complete with a uniform and a cavalry of nuns whose life work was dedicated to redeeming lost souls like me.

It was easy to meld in with the other girls. We dressed alike, walked alike and acted alike. It was demanded that we did. There was no room for individualism. And for the first time in my life, I felt as if I belonged. I was no longer the odd one, but simply one of many.

I suppose those four years were the beginning of the changes, the awakenings for me. It was during that time that I began to look not only at my own body, but compare mine to the other girls in school, especially in the locker room when we changed for gym. Even with the ever-watchful eyes of the nuns zeroed in on our every move, there were some that they missed. Like the secret touches, the looks and smiles that passed between the girls.

What I found most fascinating was that these blossoming young women weren't ashamed of their bouncy breasts, their rounded behinds, bodies in all shades—from ebony to alabaster—and thick patches of pubic hair. Rather, they seemed to flaunt them and took immense pleasure in rolling up their uniform skirts has high as possible to expose as much of their young legs as they could get away with and opening an extra button on those starched white blouses, proud of their young cleavage. It didn't seem to matter that those bold girls, those sinful girls would, spend their afternoons in detention in retribution for their flagrant disregard for humility and modesty. Instead they reveled in it like a badge of honor.

I wouldn't be like them, I promised myself, saying extra Hail Marys each day in a desperate plea to keep me pure. Yet day by day, especially at night I felt the changes, the tingles, the urges that would creep through my body like a sneaky thief leaving me shaken and confused. I'd awaken in the morning with a sticky dampness between my legs. I'd dream things, sinful things, things that made me moan in my sleep, wake up in a tangle of sheets.

The dreams were so vivid, so real. I would see myself walking down a long corridor. It was always dark, or near dark. Shadows danced along the walls. Soft music played against a background of what sounded like rushing water. But I wasn't afraid.

The closer I drew to the door at the end of the corridor, the more my body would tingle as if a million tiny fingertips played along the surface of my skin. I was naked, but I wasn't ashamed. Rather, I was proud. I was beautiful.

My feet padded silently down the corridor until I reached the door. The music, the sound of water grew. I turned the knob and opened the door. The room was dimly lit by a smattering of candles, giving the illusion of early evening. There were no windows and only one door. In the center of the room was an exquisite bed draped in layers of white chiffon, with a tumble of pillows that resembled puffs of cotton sprung from a box.

I stepped inside and closed the door behind me, looked around, not knowing who or what to expect. I moved toward the bed, instinctively knowing that it was for me. I lay down, and seemed to sink into the softness.

The chiffon brushed over me, caressed my bare skin, tweaked my nipples, slipped between my thighs and stroked my bud. I raised my knees, spread them wider, needing to feel more of the tantalizing sensation. My hips would rise and rotate as my hands traveled along the tautness of my belly up to the tender rise of my breasts. My nipples felt like pebbles beneath my palms and jolts of electricity would shoot through my body as I rubbed my hands back and forth, touching, taunting, kneading.

The chiffon pressed between my spread thighs didn't feel as soft anymore, a stiffness, a firmness had taken its place, pressing, rubbing making my bud rise, my pussy vibrate, my juices flow.

Tremors rushed through me as I pushed harder and faster against the pressure between mylegs. I wanted...something.... something more...something filling...filling me. I didn't understand it, I only knew that I needed it.

Maybe if I spread my legs wider, raised my hips higher, move them faster I would find this illusive thing that I was certain was close, close enough to smell. The pulsing began deep in my belly, down through my wet tunnel snapping it opened and closed in short, hot bursts that sprung through my limbs tensing every muscle until I was sure they would snap. I opened my mouth to suck in air as the shudders rushed through me again and again until I lay limp, spent.

There was a knock at the door. I tried to focus. Slowly, I opened my eyes. My familiar room surrounded me. A pillow was trapped between my thighs, slick in spots with my juice. My heart still raced. The knock came again. It was my mother—time to get up for school.

Did the other girls feel the same things? I wondered as I gazed around at all the studious faces buried between the pages of their textbooks. Did the bud between their legs pulse and jump late at night, when they saw someone share a kiss, hold hands or caress? Did the slick, sticky liquid slide from between their pussys when they touched their hardened nipples and imagined a boy's hand there instead?

I was afraid to touch myself in that dark place, that place that longed for something I couldn't explain. Instinctively I knew that once I did, once I crossed that thin line there would be no turning back. The dreams, the continuous volcanic sensations continued to haunt me.

What was most difficult of all during those early years was that I had no one with whom I could share my thoughts, my fears. Until I met Janet.

Janet was wild and uninhibited, and there was no punishment severe enough to curtail her antics. She was caught smoking in the girls' bathroom one afternoon, and had somehow smuggled a boy from our brother school into the confessional where they were caught tongue kissing. It was the biggest scandal, and her reputation among the other girls only elevated her to sainthood. They looked up to Janet, tried to emulate her. She had a throng of followers who viewed her as their messiah.

It never occurred to me that someone like Janet would look my way, say a word to me. I was out of her league. I was wrong.

We'd just left the cafeteria after study hall when Janet stopped me on the way out, all big smiles and protruding tits.

"Your name is Margaret, right?" She told me more than asked.

My eyes darted left then right certain she must have me confused with someone else.

"Damn nuns got you so scared, you don't even know your own name." She laughed, an intriguing kind of throaty laugh that I'd heard movie stars use just before they closed the bedroom door.

I smiled awkwardly wanting to get away, suddenly feeling a strange kind of heat in her presence.

"You're in my bio class," she stated. "I hate bio, but you're damn good at it."

"T-thanks."

"You're always by yourself. Why?"

I was trying to figure out if she were really interested or only wanted to stall for time before going to her next class: bio.

I shrugged. "Don't know, really." I shrugged again, and pushed my glasses farther up on my nose. "Just the way it is, I guess."

"Don't you ever get lonely, need somebody to talk to?"

She was really staring at me now, and I noticed what incredible sable-brown eyes she had, with a tiny mole right on the corner of her mouth that looked wet and juicy all the time.

"Sometimes."

She paused a moment, looked me up and down, but not in a condescending way, more like an evaluation.

"Maybe you'd like to hang out sometime, go to the mall or a movie or something."

Again her tone didn't sound like a question.

"I, uh, guess." My heart started racing, certain that this was one of her many pranks, and I was the unwitting victim.

"Cool."

She dug into her backpack and pulled out her notebook, jotting down her home number and ripped the page from the book then handed it to me. I stared at it for a moment, waiting for it to erupt into flames like the burning bush did with Moses. But it didn't.

"Call me sometime." She smiled and sauntered off.

I stood there for a moment, while young nubile bodies brushed by me, a lush breast on an arm, a firm hip bumping against mine, warm breath breezing by my cheek.

For days I carried around Janet's number, undecided about whether I should use it. Finally, one day after school I picked up the phone and dialed.

"Hello?"

I started to hang up, but at the last second I changed my mind-and my life.

"Hi, this is Margaret."

"Hey, Margaret."

I heard the push of air and knew she was smoking a cigarette, and wondered if her parents knew or cared.

"Whatsup?" she asked as if we always chatted on the phone.

I settled down in a chair and tried to think of something hip to say. "Nothing much, just getting ready to do my homework."

She laughed that husky laugh again. "That's what I admire about you, Margaret. You're really into your books and studying. I wish I could be more like you."

I was stunned. Speechless. More like me? Obviously, she was teasing. No one wanted to be like me, at least not on purpose. She must have been reading my mind.

"I know you probably think I'm bullshitting you, but it's true. I just can't get into this school thing."

I swallowed. "So...what do you like?"

"Music, shopping and boys. Not necessarily in that order." She laughed.

I laughed, too, and began to relax a bit. "Do...you have a boyfriend?" I dared to ask.

"Of course. How else would I get my stuff taken care of?"

"Stuff?"

"Yeah, you know...stuff."

I pretended that I did. "Ohhhh, yeah." I laughed nervously.

"Hey listen, I gotta go, Margaret. My man is at the door. Want to get a quickie before my folks get home. Talk to you tomorrow in school."

She hung up the phone and was gone, leaving me with the strong feeling that Janet was going to play a major role in my life. As I wandered back toward my bedroom, I wondered what kind of things Janet's man would do to her.

I took a deep breath and looked at Anthony. He was staring intently at me as if he was trying to see inside my soul.

"Your youth explains so many things about you...Jade. There were so many inhibitions, constraints. But we're going to remove them one by one. Tell me, how did you feel when you saw the other young women naked in the showers and in the locker rooms?"

"I-I enjoyed looking at them. I tried to see how much like them I was. I-I think it helped me in a way not to feel so odd...so bad about my body...ashamed."

Anthony nodded and made some notes. "Your dream even as a young girl interests me. It says even then that you had passion, desires. But they remained bound inside you. Your dreams were a form of release for you, if only partially. Do you still have these dreams, Jade?"

"Sometimes. Sometimes it's the same place, the same bed. Other times it's a different room and the furnishings are different." I looked across at him. "But I'm always alone."

"Because you have no real-life experience to replace the feel of the chiffon, the feel of a pillow between your legs. You want something there...the feel of a man's cock."

My face burned, and I lowered my gaze.

"Don't be ashamed of your feelings. Embrace them. Welcome them." He came from behind his desk, and I immediately noticed his erection. He didn't seem to care. "I'd like to talk about Janet some more when we meet next time. We'll pick up from there."

Anthony was right in front of me now. His erection was at the level of my mouth. I had the overwhelming urge to release it from the confines of his slacks and take it, experience the texture of it, the hardness of it.

He reached out and brushed aside a strand of loose hair. Anthony was all man, every incredible inch of him. He was the kind of man I imagined bumping and grinding between my legs. A sudden tremor raced through my body.

"Cold?" he asked.

I stood up quickly, too quickly. He was so close that the length of my body experienced the full power of his erection, which stroked me from my head to my belly. Anthony seemed unmoved. He stood there, enjoying it in that controlled way of his.

My throat was completely dry. My heart was racing. Would he kiss me, tempt me with his lips?

"I want you to think about digging deeper into your past," Anthony said in a gentle whisper. "Resurrect those early memories. And then you can share them with me. Only me."

I looked into his eyes. "Yes, I will."

"And I want to do something different next week—an experiment."

"What kind of experiment?"

He grinned. "More like a surprise. But I think you'll like it, and I'm sure it will help you even further."

"Can't you give me a hint?"

He brushed the tip of my nose with his finger. "That would ruin the surprise. I'll meet you Wednesday at six. Plan to be out for a few hours."

I stood there, waiting for more.

He returned to his desk and sat down. "I'll see you Wednesday, Jade. I have another patient in a few minutes."

That was his way of telling me in no uncertain terms that I had to leave. I picked up my purse from the chair, glanced at him one last time and walked out.

That night I could barely sleep, and when I did, my dreams were filled—haunted almost—with visions of Anthony. Anthony's hard, naked body against mine. His strong hands stroking every inch of my body. And then suddenly I saw myself standing outside of my dream, watching Anthony make wild love to another woman, a woman whose face I could not see. Some other patient, some other woman who knew exactly what to do with a man like Anthony. Some woman who had traveled the same road with him to awakening the full power of her sexuality.

I wanted to be that one, the one who writhed and bucked against him.

And I would.

Chapter Three

hen I went to work the following day, I sought out Lynn. She was in the staff lounge having her morning cup of coffee. She smiled when I walked into the room. As usual Lynn was stylishly dressed. Her makeup and hair were perfect, her skirt as short as she could manage, her long bronzed legs shimmering beneath her hose.

I took a seat beside her. There were two other secretaries hovering around, trying to kill time before returning to the drudge of the day's work. They really didn't notice me, or rather I should say they ignored me.

"Hey, girl," Lynn greeted, patting me on the thigh. "What's up? You look stressed, and it is much too early in the day." She laughed lightly.

"I was, uh, wondering…if you didn't have plans, maybe we could go to lunch."

Her face brightened as if I'd given her a surprise gift. "Sure. I usually go at one. Is that cool for you?"

I nodded. "One is fine."

"Meet you out front?"

I nodded. "Yeah. See you then." I got up and walked out. The first step of my plan was in process.

Lynn and I went to a neighborhood café near the job. The place was pretty busy when we arrived, but it didn't take long to get seats. We got a corner table near the window, and I was happy we were out of earshot of the other diners.

"So what's going on?" Lynn quizzed the instant the waitress finished taking our orders. "I've been asking you to lunch for months but you've always said no. Why the big three-sixty?"

I hesitated a moment, trying to find the best way to explain myself. All morning I'd thought about what I was going to say. I thought I had it all worked out in my head. And now my tongue was glued to my mouth.

"Are you sick, or…in trouble?" Lynn asked, her eyes reflecting her concern.

I shook my head. "No, no nothing like that." I took a sip of water. There was no way I could keep stalling so I just dived in. "I want to know…how to get a man to…" I stopped and started again. "There's this guy, uh, we met a few weeks ago and…"

"You really like him, and he doesn't return the feelings," she said, cutting me off.

I swallowed. "Something like that. I'm not really sure, actually." I couldn't tell her everything: the way we met, the conversations we've had and definitely not about what Anthony was getting me to do.

"Have you told him how you feel?"

"No."

"What do you think would happen if you did?"

He'd probably say it was part of the treatment, I wanted to tell her but didn't. "I'm not sure. I guess what I really want to know is, how can you tell if a man is interested in you or…you know…"

"Screwing you?"

"Yes."

Lynn laughed. "Honey, sometimes it's one and the same thing. If you get lucky he might see you for your mind." She laughed again.

"I guess what I really want to know is would you help me...to...make myself better—more appealing?"

"Girl, you've come to the right place." She leaned closer and lowered her voice. "First thing is to get rid of those ugly-ass glasses."

I smiled inside. Little did Lynn know that what she was helping me to become was more of the Jade than Anthony could have ever dreamed.

I met Lynn after work that day, and our first stop was the eye glass store.

"I really can't do the contact thing," I insisted, when I'd taken my number and sat down to wait. "Don't think I can deal with sticking something in my eyes every day." I gazed around.

"It's really not that bad. You should at least try it."

I shook my head. "That's out."

Lynn blew out a breath. "Okay, well let's look at some of the designer lenses."

We walked over to the display counter, and I saw several pair that I liked, but I couldn't believe the prices. They were astronomical.

"Are they kidding?" I asked, turning to Lynn. "These prices are just for the frames."

"If you want to look good, you've got to pay the cost." She angled her head to the side and waited for my decision.

I stared at the selection again. "Fine. I'll try the Fendi's," I conceded.

"Great choice," Lynn agreed, beaming with delight.

A little more than an hour later, I walked out with the beginning of my new look.

That weekend I met Lynn in midtown Manhattan, and we went in and out of more stores than I could count developing my new wardrobe. By Sunday, I was exhausted and broke, but when I gazed at the array of new finery that lay on my bed, I was truly satisfied.

Lynn couldn't understand why I wouldn't wear any of my new

things to work, and I didn't explain, only saying that there was a time and place for everything. I thanked her for all of her help and maintained my persona of plain old Margaret at the office. But underneath, Jade was burning to get out.

My practice run came that Tuesday evening. And the thrill of it still gives me tingles. I would have plenty to tell Anthony when I saw him again.

Chapter Four

*A*fter work that Tuesday, I went straight home. My nerves were strung tight. I took a quick shower, lathering myself in the vanilla-scented bath gel I'd purchased over the weekend. For tonight, Ivory soap wouldn't do. My skin glistened with the same scented body oil. It was a soft, but alluring aroma, just enough to tantalize.

I looked at the dresses hanging in my closet, the black dress among them. I smiled, and finally selected a red Lycra dress that clung to me like a second skin. The moment I slipped it on over my Victoria Secret undies, complete with G-string panties, an undeniable surge of electricity rocketed through my veins. My nipples stood as erect as twin peaks.

I faced myself in the mirror and was stunned by the transformation. Jade stood before me, sensual and ready. I had to hurry, the sun was beginning to dip below the horizon. Twilight was coming.

I took a cab to the West Village, a niche community in Manhattan where anything goes, and anything is possible. Couples come in an assortment of flavors, and the trendy restaurants and clubs were the perfect forum for my entrée.

Getting out of the cab on St. Marks, I strolled casually down the avenue with Lynn's hypnotic walk in my stride, acclimating myself to the feel and power of being Jade.

I caught the glances of many on my maiden stroll, and it filled me with a sense of challenge. I wanted to take it a step further. Finding a small, intimate bar, I went inside and took a seat at the counter.

"What will it be, Miss?" the bartender asked, wiping the space in front of me with a damp cloth.

I thought quickly. Margaret would drink ginger ale, but Jade would have something more exotic.

"Why don't you recommend something," I said, in a husky voice that I'd cultivated for the night.

He looked at me with a slight gleam in his eye. A slow smile curved his full lips. He leaned forward on the counter, resting his forearms on the wooden surface. "I'd say a lady like you would love my very special Cosmopolitan."

I returned his smile. "Then I'll try it."

While he mixed my drink, I looked around at the dimly lit space. Many of the tables were already taken and more people continued to flow inside. Music played from some unseen source and tinkling laughter could be heard between the notes. And then I saw her. Amber.

She'd just come out of the ladies' room and was returning her lipstick to her small purse. Tonight she wore black with a dip in the front that was only inches above her navel. Her dark hair flowed around her face, resembling a smoky halo. She had the walk of a cat—slinky and precise, head held high, looking neither left nor right—as if she knew she commanded the attention of everyone in the room.

I watched her progress across the floor, in between the tightly placed tables and chairs, and it seemed as if her body caressed each object she passed. She was liquid in motion. I was certain someone, some man waited for her, but she sat alone. Several unattached men came up to her, tried to engage her in conversation. She dismissed them all with a slight smile—a smile that seemed to hint at possibility.

"Here's your drink, pretty lady," the bartender said.

I blinked, shaken out of the trance that Amber's sudden appearance had put me in. "T-thank you."

Tentatively I raised the glass to my lips, tasting the rose-colored drink. I was surprised by the smooth, almost fruity taste of it. I turned around on the barstool, searching for her, but like morning mist, Amber was gone. I looked toward the door and caught a fleeting glimpse of her as she passed the glass front. For an instant she turned, our gazes connected, and she smiled at me, that smile that hinted of possibility.

My clit suddenly throbbed, and I could feel it swell. Heat coursed through me. I started to go after her, stop her, find out what it was that she knew, what secret she kept. If she would share it. But I wasn't certain I was ready to find out.

That night I dreamed the same dream again, only more intense, more real. But instead of the soft fabric of the chiffon stroking my naked body, weaving its way in and out of my thighs, taunting my sex, it was Amber's long fingers that caressed me...and Anthony's cock that pressed against my cat, trying to force it open and find that hidden place inside me. Over and over the dream possessed me throughout the night, becoming more vivid each time. The chiffon drapes bound themselves to my wrists and ankles while Amber and Anthony tormented my body. I heard my cries even in my sleep, but there was nothing I could do to stop them. I didn't want to. I wanted release. Sweet release. I begged them, pleaded with them, and they laughed, increasing the torment. Hands and tongues were everywhere at once, I was sure I would go mad. And then I felt it, the tightening of my cat, the vibrations that pumped through me like wildfire, quaking my entire body as it thrashed against the bed of downy soft-pillows.

I opened my mouth to scream as the final spasm tore through me, and my eyes sprung open, certain I would find Amber and Anthony standing above me, satisfaction brimming in their eyes and my juices on their lips.

But I was alone, with my fingers buried deep in my cat, my flow dripping down my fingertips.

Shaken and weak, I stumbled from the bed. It was 7:00 A.M. I turned on the shower, rinsing away all traces of my night from my body but not from my mind. When I stepped out of the shower, wrapped in a towel and smelling of Ivory soap, I looked in the mirror. Margaret was still intact, but Jade raged beneath, coming closer to the surface each day. I smiled, turned away from my reflection and prepared for my day.

It was Wednesday. I would see Anthony. And he had a surprise for me.

When I arrived at the building that housed Anthony's office, it was with a sense of anticipation. I had so much to tell him since our last session. I hoped he would be pleased…and maybe he would see me beyond just another patient, as a woman who desired him.

As usual the door to suite 1527 was open. I walked in and shut the door behind me. As I moved through the reception area, I wondered if there was ever anyone who worked there. With each visit, the rooms became more surreal to me. They weren't simply finely furnished rooms, but doorways that led to things unseen. How many had passed through them, been transformed in some way?

I pushed open the door to Anthony's inner office, his sanctum. The last person I expected to see sitting in the seat that should be mine was Amber.

Chapter Five

Anthony rose from the seat behind the desk, all smiles and walked toward me, hands outstretched. Amber crossed her legs, lowered her head and stared at her clasped fingers. This was the Amber I'd first seen through the window of the boutique, the woman who seemed so alone and out of place, the woman like me. Gone was the sexy siren that moved like fire, scorching everyone and everything in her path. What strange game was being played?

My eyes darted back and forth between the two of them. Did she feel about Anthony that way that I did? Had she made her dreams a reality? And what about him? What of his feelings? Did he even have any, or was all this only part of the job?

I wanted to run, to scream, to cry. I felt betrayed even though I had no reason to. In my mind, he belonged to me. What I was doing, what I was becoming was just as much for me as for him. But he had another. I was simply one of...how many?

"Jade." He clasped my shoulders. "I'm glad to see you." He placed a light kiss on my brow. "How are you since we last spoke?"

"Is this the surprise?" I tossed at him, the anger boiling inside me.

He frowned slightly. "Yes." He lowered his voice. "It's not what you think."

"You don't know what I think," I said from between my teeth. My whole body was shaking.

"Don't I?"

My gaze connected with his, and I saw the reality of his words dancing there, taunting me. Yes, he did know me. He knew and understood things about me I had yet to discover, and suddenly it frightened me.

"Please, Jade, come in and sit down. There is so much we have to do."

Amber was watching us. She smiled shyly then lowered her head again.

I pulled away from Anthony and took a seat on the far side of the room.

"I believe the two of you have met...in a way." He looked from one of us to the other. "Jade, this is Amber."

The mention of her name, the name I'd given her, said by Anthony, stunned me like a slap. I blinked rapidly.

"In Amber's other life, she is Amanda," he said, looking directly at me. "And Jade is known as Margaret."

"Nice to meet you," Amber said in a voice so soft, she could barely be heard.

"You, too," I mumbled, not sure if it were true or not.

"I've been working with Amber for six months. Why don't you tell Jade a little bit about yourself, Amber, and why you're here."

Her dark eyes darted around the room for a moment, seemingly unsure about fulfilling Anthony's request.

"It's all right," Anthony assured. "Jade is a friend." He turned toward me. "Isn't that right?"

I swallowed. I didn't know how much of a friend I was, but I did know that I wanted to find out just what was going on, and most of all the extent of the relationship between Amber and Anthony.

"Yes," I finally said in response to his question. I settled back in my seat to listen.

The room seemed to descend to another level of silence. It hovered around us waiting to be filled.

Slowly, Amber began to talk.

"When I was growing up I was always teased because I was so tall and skinny and wore thick glasses. I didn't have any friends, so I kept to myself."

"Sounds like me," I said, my hard feelings for her beginning to soften. "Did you have…fantasies?"

She pressed her lips together and stole a glance at Anthony. He nodded for her to continue.

"Yes…always," she said breathlessly. "But I didn't have anyone to talk to, no one who would understand my confusion, my needs."

"What did you do about it?" I asked.

"I learned how to pleasure myself," she confessed.

How many hours had I done the same thing even as the guilt of my act hung over me, dampening my pleasure? The fierce warnings from the nuns and stern admonitions from the priests played havoc with my mind and my conscience, but I couldn't help myself. If I were going to be damned to hell for all eternity, I wanted at least some pleasure here on earth.

"Go on, Amber," Anthony encouraged.

Amber went on to tell of her lonely childhood, her feelings of always being odd, different from the other girls in school. And the more she spoke, the more affinity I felt for her. There was so much about us that was alike. The acceptance of that reality began to disturb me the more she talked. Did she, too, feel the same way about Anthony as I did? Did he return those feelings? Had she gotten from him what I desired?

"… and then I met, Anthony," she was saying. "Everything changed for me."

A look passed between them that was too personal for my tastes. I had a good mind to leave them to their erotic games. But I couldn't. I wanted to know it all. And I wanted to prove to Anthony that I, Jade, was what he needed. I envisioned my sexy undergarments beneath my clothes. I wanted him to see me in them. I wanted him to see me without them. So I stayed.

"I thought that we would spend the evening together," Anthony announced. "I've made reservations for dinner." He looked from one of us to the other. "But we have a short excursion first."

"Is this your idea of group therapy," I snapped.

Anthony smiled. "It's a way of looking at it. And I think it will do you both good. I want to see you both out in the world."

Amber remained quiet, going along with the program without a peep.

"Fine," I finally mumbled.

"My car is downstairs." He headed for the door and held it open.

Amber walked out first without a backward glance. As I passed him, I stopped for a moment, looked into his eyes, hoping to see some answers there. All I found was a steamy darkness, bottomless mystery and the sensuous smile that played around his mouth.

I was unsure what the night would hold for the three of us, but I had every reason to believe that it would be an awakening. One way or the other.

I was mildly surprised that Anthony had a driver, which upon reflection worked well. All during the ride that night, he was able to devote his attention to us, and the close proximity of the three of us, secluded in the cool confines of soft leather, only enhanced the simmering heat that snapped and popped among us.

Anthony pushed a button and a small bar opened. He poured us each a glass of white wine. "To you, ladies, and to the exciting future that awaits you," he said, toasting us.

Our glasses clinked in unison.

Anthony leaned back, appraising us both, then he turned those dangerous eyes and disarming smile on me. I felt my cat contract in instant response.

"When we last spoke, Jade, we talked about your youth and your friend Janet. I want to finish that conversation."

"Here? Now?" My eyes flashed toward Amber, who seemed unflustered by his request.

"If we are going to make progress, we must shed our inhibitions." He leaned closer. I could smell his maleness. "Don't be afraid or ashamed, Jade. Amber was just like you once, trapped inside herself, unable to share. But she's changed." He looked at Amber.

"Haven't you, Amber?"

She smiled a sly, seductive smile and a light seemed to simmer behind her eyes. "Yes," she answered in a throaty whisper.

A shiver ran up my spine as I watched the subtle transformation right in front of my eyes. Although at first look she appeared dowdy, closer inspection revealed the fever, the allure that seemed to seep from her pores. It was in the tilt of her head, the languid way her body seemed to drape across the leather seat, the posture of a woman who understood the true power of her sex.

"Go on, Jade," she said, her voice like a caress. "Tell us."

I hesitated a moment, trying to digest what I'd just seen, understand the full implications of it all. I pulled in a breath and picked up where I'd left off.

I'd finished another day at school, where the nuns preached all day about sin and damnation. "Impure actions, impure thoughts will never get you into heaven," they reminded us daily. Them in their ominous black robes, hands hidden in the cowls of their sleeves—touching themselves, I'm sure now, between the folds of midnight. Bad thoughts, bad actions would be punished, they'd say. "Purity is next to godliness."

Pure, I mused, stepping outside into the cool afternoon. *I will be pure and holy. Free of sin, bad thoughts and actions.* Trapped in my thoughts of righteousness and redemption I slowly walked along the street thinking more about the lessons of the day. Heading for home and more of the sameness, I had a sudden change of heart. Earlier Janet had invited me to stop by her house, hang out for a while. "It'll be fun," she'd insisted. "We could listen to some music, talk...you know." She grinned. I told her I'd think about it. She wrote her address on a slip of paper and handed it to me. "If you decide to come, just drop by. I'll be there," she said and sauntered off.

I dug in my knapsack for her address. She lived close to the school. Only another two blocks. I really didn't feel like going home.

Changing direction I headed for Janet's house, and what was to be another stunning eye-opener.

When I reached her house I rang the front doorbell and waited. No one answered. I tried one more time and that's when I realized the door was slightly open. Gingerly, I stepped inside and called her name.

I heard noises, movement coming from upstairs and figured that she was in her room. I headed for the stairs. When I reached the landing moans drifted to me from the partially opened doorway of Janet's bedroom. My heart raced. Janet was moaning, in pain, I believed. I should have run, called someone. I didn't. There was something about the sounds that were both frightening and thrilling at the same time. Something decadent, almost sinful. What is sin in the flesh? I wanted to see it.

I eased closer to the door, my pulse pounding, and there they were, silhouetted against the waning light. A man's dark, muscled body was atop Janet's smaller one, her legs stretched wide on either side of him, her breasts were pressed flat beneath his chest. He moved up and down on her, in and out of a place I could not see—only imagine.

She moaned loudly, her eyes closed, sweat dripping from his face onto her face, which was twisted—in pain or pleasure, I couldn't be certain.

The man's large hands clamped around Janet's butt, pulling her tighter against him until their bodies seemed as one. Her mouth opened in an *O*, each moan and sigh freed with his each and every thrust.

"That's it, baby. Give it to me like you mean it," he murmured in a ragged voice. "Give it to Daddy."

The bed creaked and groaned in response to every plunge of him into Janet, who buried her sweating face in a pillow. Her arms were wrapped around his tapered back as if she were drowning, so tight that I saw the strain of the muscles and sinews in them.

I stood there, paralyzed by the sight in front of me, animalistic and fascinating in all of its sinfulness. The shock of the forbidden scene rooted me to my spot at the door. I could not move if I wanted to.

"Oh, God," Janet shouted. "Oh, God!" She raised her legs higher up his back as if trying to climb a tree, the muscles of her thighs tensing, her fingers buried in his dark flesh.

Heat infused me, my head pounded and a throb began to beat between my legs. I trembled all over, and I heard my own whimpered moans mix with theirs. I was frightened. But I couldn't tear my gaze away. Instead, I lifted the navy blue skirt of my uniform and slipped a finger down into my panties to still the beating, find its source. Something wet and sticky slid across my fingertip, and I gasped in fear. What had I done? What was happening to me? I couldn't stop. Didn't want to. I pressed my fingers harder, faster, matching their rhythm, which had picked up a fevered almost frenzied pitch. Their words to each other assaulted my ears, intensified my own frantic search for—what I couldn't be sure.

"Pussy."

"More."

"Right there."

"God, help me."

"Take it."

"This is mine."

"It's yours. Always."

My one finger became two, slipping and sliding over the bud of my sex, feeling it swell and harden until it felt as if it would explode in delight. Sensations that I'd never known before swept through me, weakening my legs, exploding one by one in my head. I wanted so badly to stop but I couldn't. It was wrong, touching myself like that. I couldn't stop. What would Sister Broderick say if she saw me?

Then suddenly the man's voice sounded as if he was strangling, a deep guttural moan filled the room and his body stiffened as if electrified. Janet's cries sounded like one being tortured as her body shook violently, her head thrashing back and forth on the soaked pillow. And then they lay still. The only sounds in the room were their deep, labored breathing, the one thing that made me realize that they were not dead—dead for what they had done.

He finally rolled off Janet, and for the first time I see a man's cock. It is still erect and throbbing, dark and dangerous-looking, pointing to the ceiling. And I wondered how she was able to take that inside of her, let it fill her, slide in and out of her. Didn't it hurt? Didn't it rip that tight little hole open?

But she was smiling. Smiling as if this—what had been done to her—was the most wonderful experience in her life. She lay there beside him, eyes closed, legs still arched and spread. And I wondered if my pussy looked like hers—pink, wet. The scent of them filled my nostrils, the mysterious aroma of sex and lust, and sent my own pussy into another wave of convulsions until my legs tremble, uncontrollably. For a moment, I shared what Janet must have felt and that thought fed my guilt and shame.

Fascinated by what I had seen, confused by what I'd been taught, shaken by what my own body cried out for, I quietly tiptoed away, closing the door behind me to finish what I'd begun standing in the hallway outside of Janet's room. Could sin be so bad if it made your body feel so good, I wondered as my fingers slipped faster in and out of my pussy. My moans were muffled by the fist I pushed against my mouth, just as I'd seen Janet do, until that first shot of release erupted in a terrifying surge that arched my hips toward the ceiling—wanting more, again and again.

And that's how it started—my search for satisfaction. It was my secret. I couldn't tell anyone of the sinful, erotic things that went through my mind, the dirty little tricks I did to my body in the darkness of my room.

To all who knew me, I was and am Margaret—quiet and unassuming by day. Listening to the nuns, my parents, all those in authority. But under the cloak of night I seek release—and find it—always, in one way or another. And I felt delightfully sinful.

I took a breath, trying to push that day to the back of my mind.

Even now, years later, every time I think of it, envision it, I get hot and cream in my panties. In the car with Anthony and Amber was the first time I'd told anyone of that afternoon. And even with all the time Janet and I spent together I'd never uttered a word.

"How did seeing your friend having sex make you feel?" Anthony asked.

"Anthony, the vision of them having sex stayed with me for years and more than once I thought about approaching Father O' Toole after Vespers to speak to him about what I'd seen. But something inside me, maybe my conscience, wouldn't let me. At sixteen, I was so curious about sex and obsessed about what men and women did together, but the guilt that accompanied those horny thoughts prevented me from acting on any of my feelings."

"Do you think you...had a thing for women?" Amber asked, her right hand pressed hard between her thighs.

I swallowed. "No. Not really. It was just that I had no males that were interested in me at the time. I suppose I had some sort of fascination with women, but it wasn't to have sex with them, but more to discover what they knew."

Anthony nodded slowly. "That's quite understandable, especially in one so young at the time with no experience and no outlet for your feelings. Combine that with the type of life you were living and the religious guilt that was heaped upon you at school and at home, it's no wonder you were so confused."

"Did anything...ever happen with you and Janet?" Amber quizzed. "She sounds like an interesting young woman. I wish I would have known someone like her."

I looked at Amber oddly. Her eyes had taken on a feverish hue. She was really turned on by my tale. I smiled inside. I wanted to see just how far she would go if I told her the rest.

I leaned back against the leather and continued my story.

One late afternoon in December, I went to Janet's house after school. Her father was a cop and her mother, a large woman with enormous breasts and drumstick legs, worked for a realty company in the city. Janet took after her mother. She had a very big chest for a girl her age. Larger even than my mother—36C. Although she was quiet like myself around adults, she was a wildcat around the girls at school and had a reputation. Very pretty and very crazy. I was proud to be her friend. She did things I could only dream about doing.

"Have you ever gone all the way?" Janet asked me that afternoon while sitting on the bed in her room. "Have you ever let a boy put it in you?"

I blushed, thankful for the setting sun, the hint of twilight creeping into the room. "No...I can't do that." I remembered that afternoon I saw her and that man, and I immediately got hot all over.

She laughed at my discomfort, not knowing what it really stemmed from and flicked a strand of hair away from her copper-tinged face and leaned back against the bed rest. "I have. Not with the stupid boys from around here, but with a real man. An older man. A friend of my father. He took his time, he didn't rush like these little boys do. I thought I'd pass out when he put his lips to my breasts, licked them. My nipples get hard just thinking about what he did to me."

"Your father's friend?" I'm shocked but I glanced down at the front of her starched white blouse and see the swollen buds of her breasts straining against the fabric.

"Have you ever had sex at all?" Janet stared at me strangely as she walked to the door and twisted the lock, insuring our privacy. My heart flutters because I don't know what will happen next. Janet was capable of anything.

Anthony pulled out his pad and wrote something down, looked at me with a half smile, then went back to his notes. "So what did this Janet do next? Remember, don't leave anything out. I want to know everything, every detail. The only way I can help you is to understand the origins of your sexual awakening."

Well, Janet came back to the bed but she didn't sit down. Instead, she stopped for a minute, watching me with this queer look; then she started undressing before me until she didn't have a stitch on. Nothing. I'd seen girls naked before, in the shower at school, but somehow this was different. She thought nothing of showing herself to me. Was I excited? Sure, I was. That throbbing between my legs, which I'd first felt that day I saw her and that man doing it came back, and I couldn't take my eyes off her.

"Now you take your clothes off, Margie," Janet said to me in a strange, raspy voice. I just sat there for a time, not knowing what to think. This was a real sin, two girls together. A Cardinal sin, a violation of the Holy Text beyond all redemption.

Yet, I did as she asked and removed all of my clothes until I was standing naked before her lusty eyes. She laughed when I folded them all neatly and placed them in an orderly stack on a chair.

"Did you know that you have a really hot body, girl?" she said, staring first at my breasts, which were not nearly as big as hers and then at my curly haired crotch.

For some reason, I felt my nipples start to get hard. Janet, looking deep into my eyes, stepped close to me and touched my shoulders, down along the smooth skin of my arms and finally my breasts, cupping them, circling the roundness of them with delicate strokes of her long, elegant fingers. When I flinched, she laughed that bold laugh of hers and teased me to lighten up.

What happened next? Oh, God, where do I start? It was as if I was in this trance, in a fog, watching myself from outside my body. She leaned forward and placed her warm lips on my nipples, sucking on them softly but urgently until I thought I would go crazy with desire, her tongue flicking back and forth like a snake's over the sensitive nubs of each breast. I don't know how much time went by as she worked slowly on them, sending this incredible heat through my body. Even my blood felt hot. In that same raspy voice, she said, with her mouth close to my ear, "Lay back on the bed and open it up for me." I thought about what I was doing for a panicky moment and imagined the Holy Mother was looking down on us and frowning at the loss of another soul.

I never knew a woman could make me feel like that. I can still hear her whispering to me, *yes, yes, sweetness, that's what I want,* as she gently eased me back on the bed and pulled apart my legs. *Close your eyes and just feel.*

It was all so dreamlike. Her finger entered me, then withdrew. Was this what a man's cock felt like? I opened my eyes just in time to see her bring a finger to her mouth, lick it, and bring it back down to touch that tiny bud of flesh above my opening, causing me to fall back against the bed and arch my legs. Endless wave of delicious shudders surged through me when she opened me up, inserting two fingers into the velvet wetness, teasing me with them, taunting me, and suddenly her mouth and tongue were there, too. There and everywhere until my hips were thrusting against her face wildly, grinding my cat against her hot mouth. I almost screamed out loud when her tongue shot deep inside me into a place where no man had ever been, and Holy Mother of God, my first orgasm caught me by surprise, sneaked up on me and rocked me from head to toe. Her whole mouth covered my cat and sents shocks of sensation through me, one after another, one after another, until it was hard to breathe. I thought I was going to die from cumming, two more times in a row. And then we kissed, like men and women do, her tongue tasting and licking the ridges and mounds of my lips. After we finished, I was worn out, spent, the convulsions from deep inside my cat still throbbing dangerously. Both of us were covered with sweat.

Just then there was a knock on the door. It was her father, the cop. He said something about April, another one of Janet's friends, being on the phone. Calmly, Janet told him that she'd call her back later, and we got out of bed. Without even looking at each other, we toweled off with her blouse and put on our clothes. Something important to both of us had happened, something that neither of us ever mentioned again.

Amber smiled wickedly, her skirt hiked up to her crotch. I could almost see her short and curlies. She stared at me with such lust in her eyes that I was sure if Anthony were not in the car she would have made a meal of me.

"So you do like women," she purred.

My gaze darted to Anthony. "Do you think this incident with Janet means that I've got latent lesbian tendencies? Or maybe I'm bisexual? Or just a freak?"

He took a long sip from his glass and slipped his hand beneath the notepad on his lap. His voice was tight, strained. "Margaret, a lot of girls experiment sexually at that stage or even later, but it doesn't make them this thing or that."

The notepad slipped to the floor. I glanced down between his legs. The erection throbbed tantalizingly against the fabric of his midnight-blue pants.

He wants me, I think to myself feeling elated by the discovery. *My talks with him excite him, turn him on.* It was then that I decided what I must do. He thought these sessions would help me find something, some part of myself that was lost along the way. So I'd tell him of my adventures, my flights in between the night, if only to see the hard knob of his sex reach out, yearning for me—Jade. His obsession. I smiled to myself. Anthony had no idea of the door he had opened.

Finally the car pulled to a stop, and the next episode of our adventure began.

Chapter Six

When we stepped from the car I was stunned to see that we were at the beach, a remote part of the beach on the Long Island Sound. It was exquisite. Even from our parking spot I could hear the gentle lapping of the waves, the scent of wet sand and ocean water. The dying sun cast a brilliant orange and gold band across the ripples. Why had he brought us here, I wondered, stepping out of my shoes, letting the sand tickle my toes.

"No one comes here," Anthony was saying. "We're alone, and I think the atmosphere, the seclusion is just what we need to...really open up." He smiled at us both.

My heart knocked in my chest. Was he thinking a threesome? I knew I wasn't ready for that, didn't want it. I wanted him to be the first for me. I needed that to happen, and I wouldn't share him with Amber. I just couldn't.

Anthony took my hand, bent down and whispered in my ear. "I know what you're thinking. I know what you want. I want it, too. And it will happen, when you're really ready to give yourself completely without inhibitions. And I'll be waiting. Trust me," he said before placing a kiss on my lobe. I shivered, even against the muggy heat of the night.

Anthony walked toward the car and returned shortly with his arms full. Amber walked over to him and took the rolled blanket from his arm, leaving him to carry a large wicker basket and a red-and-white cooler. They walked toward a strip of beach that they seemed drawn to as if they'd been here before—together. My mind conjured dozens of images at once: Anthony's thick cock moving in and out of Amber's slick wetness, her back outlined in the damp sand; the two of them locked as one beneath the push and pull of the waves, on the boardwalk, under the stars. The images played over and over in my head until it spun.

When I blinked them away and focused, Anthony was standing in front of me, a curious smile on his face. "Yes, it can be wonderful," he said in a way that assured me he'd read my thoughts again. "Think of all the possibilities, Jade. All of them, then take them a step higher. That's where I'll take you, Jade, to that forbidden place inside of you that has yet to fully emerge. But you've got to let go," he ended on a husky hush of a note. He reached out and stroked the curve of my jaw, let his finger drift along the arch of my collarbone, down the center of my breasts. All the air from my lungs seemed to become trapped in my throat. My heart thundered in unison with the waves that crashed against the rocks. "Let's get this evening underway. Our reservations await." He took my hand and led me to where Amber had set out a meal that looked to be catered from the finest restaurant.

The blanket had been covered with a white linen cloth. Fine dining chin,; gleaming silver, wineglasses, and candles encased in tulip-shaped goblets set the mood. There was salad, soup, a choice of braised chicken sprinkled with herbs, thumb-sized cocktail shrimp, steamed vegetables and wild or yellow rice. Dessert was a creamy blend of sorbet in raspberry, pineapple, mango and orange.

Wine flowed freely. I couldn't recall a glass being empty at any time during the evening. And as the food, the wine, the allure of the sea, began to seep into our pores, creep into our minds, shuttle through our bodies, inhibitions moved out with the tide. Our laughter, rich and heavy, echoed over the waves, bounced against the rocks and came back to join us, to taunt us, ease beneath our clothes, heating our bodies.

Amber was first. Giddy with delight, a sense of freedom, she rose from her supine position in the sand, looked at us both with a wicked gleam in her eye and began to undress.

Yes, I have to admit, I couldn't take my eyes off her. Not because she was beautiful or that I was attracted to her, but the hypnotic effect of watching her striptease and wondering if I, too, could mesmerize with a gyration of my hips, the thrust of my breasts, the cupping of my cat with hungry fingers, all under the guise of taking off my clothes, projecting images of what I could do with my body that teased and taunted the salivating spectators.

Anthony was leaning on his side, his hand propping up his head, watching, not so much with a look of fascination, but evaluation. The way a teacher studies a student's work, judging whether the lessons taught were learned and understood. He sipped his wine as Amber languidly rotated her hips, eyes closed, mouth wet while her hands roamed her body and like a magician snapped her panties into two tiny pieces of satin and tossed them into the sand.

The close-cut and trimmed hair of her pussy glimmered under the light of the moon, reflecting the dew drops of her arousal that glistened like diamonds on the hard pearl of her clit. She danced to the waves, her body becoming almost liquid.

Anthony set down his glass and turned toward me. His hand was on my thigh. "Try it, Jade," he said, his voice carrying a heavy almost gritty note. His eyes burned and sparkled in the night light. "Please," he urged. "For me. For you."

I looked quickly up at Amber who undulated now with abandon. She was totally absorbed in herself, in pushing herself along the ladder of her own private passions. Her eyes were closed, her fingers disappearing and appearing from between the wetness of her legs that slid like a drizzling rain down her brown thighs.

Anthony's hand crept farther up my thigh, stroking, caressing along the way. The tender flesh there quivered and heated beneath his fingers. A puff of air, a sigh, a moan slipped helplessly through my lips. A man's touch. A real man's touch. The one I'd dreamed of, fantasized about. I wanted to grab his hand, press it against my pussy where the heat leaped out of me in waves. I wanted it to put out the fire.

I rested back on my elbows, my raised knees dropped open— *make it easy for him,* I thought. I could feel the night breeze scoot between my tingling thighs. Anthony smiled and let his hand travel a bit farther, the pressure just a bit harder.

My breath came in short bursts like gun shots, *pop, pop, pop.* My skirt was up around my hips now. My pussy caught the full impact of the night air.

A low groan from deep in Anthony's throat burned against my flesh when he suddenly put his lips against my thighs. My head grew light. I closed my eyes certain that I would faint when I felt the pressure of his mouth pressed against my cat, the only thing separating his eager tongue from lapping the woman juice that flowed there was the thin fabric of my G-string.

"Take them off."

The request wasn't Anthony's, but Amber's. "Take them off," she purred again.

Dazed, I looked up, tried to focus. She stood above us, her fully naked body glowing in the moonlight. "Let us see," she said, her voice heavy with her own excitement and the wine. She massaged her breasts while she spoke.

I looked at Anthony who smiled in waiting. He rolled away from me. "You must decide if you will be Margaret or Jade," he said evenly. "Margaret would hesitate. Jade would capture the moment, grip it between her pussy lips and never let go until she was good and damn ready."

My head snapped back and forth between the two of them, challenge lit their eyes like twin flames.

Who would I be tonight? Yes, I'd tried to be Jade when I wandered along through the streets of Manhattan. I'd tried to be Jade when I shopped for the sexy outfits with Lynn. I tried to be Jade when I stood in front of Anthony and his hard cock was pressed against me. But this, this was different. There was no room for pretense. This was the real thing, the first test. Would I pass or fail?

Slowly, then with more determination I stood, looking at them both with a hint of challenge in my own eyes. A smile crept across my mouth. No. Amber would not win at this game.

I strolled toward the water, at first just letting the waves lap across my bare feet. I step out farther until it reached my knees, then my waist, my breasts. My dress clung to me now, outlining every curve, every dip.

I came back to them wet and wanting. I ran my hands over my drenched body pressing the fabric even closer to my skin. I watched Anthony's eyes sparkle with anticipation. Amber took a seat beside him on the blanket.

One by one I unfastened the buttons of my dress. I pulled the right side away revealing the fullness of that breast with its pebble-hard nipple. Anthony smiled. I covered myself and slowly revealed the other side. I played this game of hide-and-seek for a minute more before easing the top of the dress off my shoulders. I turned my back to them, spread my legs and bent over, easing my dress up above my hips, swaying from side to side. Anthony applauded.

Standing slowly, I wiggled out of my dress until all that stood between me and nakedness was my bra and matching G-string. When I turned, Anthony was standing right in front of me. Close enough that I could feel the warmth of his breath brush my face.

He stroked my face, removed my glasses then placed a feather-light kiss on my lips. "You're beautiful," he whispered. "More than you realize." His hand dropped down from my face to cup my breast. He squeezed gently, and I thought I'd faint with delight. He put his hand flush against my pussy and stared deep into my eyes. "You're wet. Not sea-water wet, woman wet." His fingers probed. My legs quivered. He took my hand and pressed it firmly against his erection. "Do you want this, Jade?" he whispered. "Do you want this inside of you?"

"Yes," I said on a strangled sigh. "Yes."

"Then you'll have me. And I'll have you."

He kissed me then, really kissed me for the first time. And when his tongue probed my mouth, danced with mine, lights went off in my head. My body sagged against his and he pulled me tighter, caressed my butt, pressed his hardness deep between my legs. Bolts of pleasure shot through me as he eased my bra aside and took a nipple into his mouth, sucking it as if to draw out the essence of me.

Then suddenly he stopped, eased back and looked down into my eyes. "Will you be ready for anything, anything I ask, whenever I ask?" he urged, while slipping a finger into my pussy.

I couldn't think. It took me a moment to focus on what he is saying. How could I deny him anything?

I nodded numbly, only wanting the pleasure to continue, to finish what he'd begun.

"Good." He stepped away. "On Saturday, be ready. And then you can tell me all about it when we meet again."

That's all he said before he turned and walked away and began putting our things back in the basket.

This thing between Anthony and me was turning into something that I could never imagine.

Chapter Seven

*B*ut until next Wednesday, until I could reveal myself again, I had to continue the hunt for satisfaction, bring back the spoils to share with my keeper—for us both to savor and enjoy. The decadence of what we gave each other with our erotic game of words, spurred me on to greater heights, more dangerous games like the night in the elevator...

Anthony always says every sexual experience, every adventure, has contributed to who I've become, my total self. So what does the night of my escapade in the elevator of a large downtown department store reveal about me—reveal about him? I had no idea what Anthony had in mind for Saturday, and he refused to answer any of my questions on the ride home. Amber sat by silently amused at my probing as if she already knew the answers. The mere thought of that infuriated me, made me more determined than ever to prove to Anthony, to them both that I was the one. I would get what I wanted.

The days leading up to Saturday were nerve racking. Lynn continually asked me if I was all right. That I seemed jumpy and nervous. I lied to her, told her I was having a hard time sleeping lately and was simply overtired. She seemed to accept my explanation but still gave me curious looks.

"What you need is a stiff dick," she said to me while we freshened ourselves up in the ladies' room that Friday afternoon.

I stared at her wide-eyed and innocent. "What?"

"You heard me. A good screwing would set you straight. I still can't believe we did all that shopping for all those sexy clothes, and you haven't done anything with them. How do you ever expect that man you like to notice you if you keep going around looking like a schoolmarm?" She peered in the mirror and applied another coat of red lipstick.

I couldn't even begin to tell her about the things that had been going on, the erotic games that were being played, the wild and crazy dreams I'd had, the needs that were building in me ready to explode—my other self. But I was ready for whatever the future held.

"What makes you think he hasn't noticed me?" I asked.

Lynn turned to me, her eyebrow arched in question. "Has he?"

I smiled. "Maybe he has," I said and turned away, envisioning the black crotchless panties I'd decided to wear that day. "Maybe he has." I walked out leaving Lynn with more questions than answers.

Saturday finally arrived. I was like a cat on a hot tin roof, pacing across my bedroom floor waiting for the phone to ring, some sign of what was to come. But nothing happened. As the day dragged on, my spirits sank. I hadn't heard a word from Anthony. Maybe this was just another one of his mind games.

Depressed, I decided to go to the mall. I needed to get a gift for my mother's birthday.

I dressed very casually, wearing a blouse the color of a ripe Georgia peach. But feeling incredibly horny I decided on no bra and no panties. I put on a matching long skirt that billowed around my ankles, and sandals with no back. The look, innocent yet seductive, brought me hungry stares from several men and annoyed frowns from many of the women. I smiled.

As I walked away from the perfume counter, I turned around after the salesclerk shouted that I'd left my purchase behind—an expensive bottle of Chanel No. 5. He reached over and handed me the bag, containing the gift-wrapped scent. There was a smile that had nothing to do with my faulty memory or the perfume on his freckled face, but I ignored him and walked quickly away.

Out of the corner of my eye, I saw him, dressed very coolly in an understated summer outfit, in all khaki.

I walked quickly in the other direction, with my package securely under my arm, figuring that I was safe as long as I stayed in a crowd of people. Once I thought I'd lost him, but he popped up near the escalator, standing just to the left of a woman and her three kids.

I got on. Going up. He got on right behind me. I felt the heat of his body radiate against the back of mine. He was standing much too close to me. My bare nipples immediately stood erect. Warning me.

There was no escape from him. There was nowhere for me to go, casual shoppers filled the stairs ahead of me. Suddenly, the tip of his finger slid along the line of my butt.

"Don't turn around," he whispered.

I don't look around. Afraid, but turned on. This was the longest escalator ride I'd ever been on. Maybe he'd had his fun and would get off. No, he did it again, with a bit more force this time. And my juices began to flow from my pussy and slid down my leg. At first, I was annoyed with him for doing this in a public place but soon that feeling was overcome by my rising sense of excitement.

I began to tremble as I finally stumbled off and hurried down the busy corridor.

Glancing over my shoulder, I caught a glimpse of his darkness, moving like a shadow between the tight cluster of bodies.

I hurried toward the back of the mall before I realized I was walking into an area under construction. Suddenly I was alone. I looked for the exit signs, determined not to go back the way I'd come. But I wanted to run into him again. Have him touch me again. Make me feel like that again. My skin prickled with an almost eerie anticipation. Where could I go?

I walked farther, the noise of the shoppers growing dimmer until I reached a glass-enclosed elevator on the far side of the shopping complex. I looked out of the plate-glass window and noticed how dark it had grown since I'd first arrived, hours earlier. There were still a few shoppers milling about. The stranger was nowhere in sight but I could still feel his presence. He was not far away.

I pressed the button and waited.

Finally the elevator arrived. I sighed in relief and stepped inside. As I turned to press the button, there he was, standing in front of me. Smiling. "I was hoping you'd come here."

He held his hand against the side of the door to keep it from closing. Taking his time, he stepped on. The doors shut, sealing us inside.

I moved to the back of the car, holding my precious package against my breasts, putting space between us. He didn't move for several seconds, only smiled. I had the feeling that this was not the first time he'd done something like this. When he stepped closer to me and raised one of his huge hands, I squirmed with anticipation and more juice drips from between my thighs.

"Don't hide them from me," he said in his gentlest voice. "They're beautiful. Let me see them."

He reached toward me and took the package from my numb fingers, letting it fall to the floor. I glanced at him with disapproval, and he just shrugged. Cocky bastard.

The elevator began its descent. He pressed the red button, and the elevator came to a jerking halt. His hand went to the front of his pants, stroking the long, hard bulge that twitched at his touch. He enjoyed the look of shock on my face as he used his fingers to pleasure himself right before my eyes.

"Please open your blouse. Let me look at you."

His eyes were so soft and warm, I almost felt safe—almost. They were locked on mine. I felt his power over me. I wanted to resist but couldn't. I submitted to the irrational urge of the moment, to his superior will.

One by one, I opened the tiny white buttons of my blouse. All my shyness, all of my Margaret self, evaporated and soon my breasts were in partial view. I wanted to retain some control by teasing him. But he wasn't letting me have my say in any of it.

His voice was hard and forceful this time. "Let me see them. Spread it open for me."

I did as he asked. He smiled once more like a parent satisfied with an obedient child.

He inched closer and pushed the blouse off my shoulders and down my arms. "Just as I pictured them," he murmured before feasting on one then the other and back again.

Pebbly hard nipples graze across his tongue, between his teeth, and I felt my clit swell, my lips spread. His hands rode up and down my hips, inching my skirt up to my waist, revealing the dark, wet triangle that no man had ever before seen.

I shuddered, when his fingertip teased the tip of my bud, and I knew it came away wet, slick with my juice. I couldn't take my eyes off his large cock, now forming a tent in his cool khaki pants.

He sucked my right nipple deep into his mouth, and I cried out when his teeth clamped around it in a painful kind of pleasure. He tried to push his thick finger up inside me, and I froze as an unfamiliar pain grips me.

Suddenly he stepped back, looked into the fear, the expectation in my eyes. "Fresh...pure," he said before finding the zipper to my skirt and releasing it, letting it fall into a pool at my feet.

He wrapped his arm around my waist and slid down my exposed body until he was on his knees in worship in front of me. He pressed his face to my cat. Tingles erupted inside the soft flesh of my thighs. "A virgin," he whispered softly, dropping tiny kisses in the curly hairs. He held me tighter, his arm coiling around me, as his tongue stroked my cat, licking it as a child laps a cone of ice cream.

My juices filled his mouth, dripping along the sides of his full lips. The hairs of his mustache teased the folds of my sex as his tongue dipped deeper. He squeezed my butt. Shudders raced through me. My legs weakened as the first of many climaxes that night began to build in my womb.

His arm released its hold, and with no support I slid down the cool metal wall of the elevator to the floor, my legs spread wide on either side of his face. He pushed them farther apart, straining the muscles.

134

He eased back and looked at my wet, slick pussy.

"Nice," he whispered and stroked it. "You want to become a woman—a real woman?" he asked in that gentle way of his.

I swallowed, my throat dry from stifling my cries. "Yes," I told him in a hoarse voice. "Yes, yes. Make a woman out of me."

He laughed and slid a finger up my hole, pushing until I cried out. Then two. The pain forced tears to burn my eyes. One more. My cat was on fire.

Draping my legs over his arms, he kissed the inside of my thighs. Up and down, back and forth, until the need overrode the pain.

"Make me a woman." I begged him now. He laughed. Sucked my clit again—and again.

"Touch my cock," he commanded. "Touch it. Feel what I have for you." He raised up on his knees. His cock stood out in front of him. Hard, long, dark. Bigger than anything I've seen or imagined. That thing could never fit inside me. Never.

Yet, terrified but fascinated I reached for it, wrapped my fingers around it. It jerked in my hand, jumped when I touched the tender, swollen head.

"Stroke it. Like I stroked your pussy with my tongue."

I did as he asked. Feeling the hard ridges, the veins that throbbed at my touch. His large hands covered my knees, pushed them apart so he could see my cat opening and closing—waiting.

He pulled away, out of my grasp and looked down at me with that half smile. "Lay down." I did. He stood, stepped out of his pants, then lowered himself above me. He kissed my right knee, raised it above his shoulder. He kissed my left knee and raised it to the other shoulder.

The head of his cock teased my clit—pressed against me, easy at first. He clamped the globes of my butt in the palms of his hand and pulled me toward him, raised up on his knees and pushed again and again—harder each time.

A burning pain seared my insides, flashed to my head and spread to my limbs. My entire body shuddered and the wet walls opened. He filled me, spreading me open with his cock moving in and out, then in a slow, rotating rhythm.

Soon the pain ebbed, the trembling eased and tiny waves of pleasure rolled through me with every thrust, and I felt that funny feeling building in my belly and I cried out, not from pain but from the incredible pleasure that exploded inside me.

Before I could catch my breath, he turned me over, put me on my hands and knees and took me from behind. I like that, too, and began to push my butt up against his cock every time he slammed into me. He reached around me and tickled my swollen clit with his finger, and I came again and again.

I felt so dizzy, so weak. Slowly I opened my eyes—and he was gone. The doors to the elevator were gaping open, just like my legs. I pulled myself up, adjusted my clothes and stumbled out into the night—a woman.

Anthony and I would have plenty to talk about when I saw him on Wednesday.

Chapter Eight

*L*ust filled me now, consumed me like hungry flames lapping at tinder wood. I had to put the fire out now that it had been ignited.

I bathed myself in the essence of vanilla, then smoothed scented oil on my damp skin until it glowed. Opening my closet, I searched through the array of new clothes that I'd purchased with Lynn. I picked out a micromini dress in a hot pink, matching undies and three-inch heels—they did great things for my legs. A dab of scented oil behind my ears, between my breasts and behind my knees. Lipstick was last. I dropped the tube in my purse, fluffed my hair one more time and stepped out into the night.

That night I decided to take the train downtown. I walked the three blocks to the station, looked behind me once at the presence I felt. I smiled and descended the steps.

I paid my fare and pushed through the turnstile onto the empty platform. I walked down to the far end, my heels clicking rhythmically against the gray concrete, echoing off the stone wall. I leaned against it and wait.

The sound of footsteps drew closer. My heart began to race. I felt my pussy tingle with anticipation, my nipples hardened. And then the footsteps became a shadow and the shadow became a man.

There were no words, no need for questions or introductions, just us in the dimly lit tunnel. We knew why we were there, what we wanted. He stepped closer, the warmth of his body enveloped me like a long-lost friend.

"This is where you want it?" he asked, while brushing my bottom lip with his thumb.

The idea that someone, anyone could walk up on us at any minute only excited me more.

"Yes," I whispered. "Right here."

His smile crept across his mouth. He took a quick glance down the long corridor of the platform. We were still alone.

I pushed aside the folds of his black trench coat and stroked his chest, then the taut muscles of his stomach. I felt bold, daring. I felt Jade.

My fingers, which for years were only nimble on the keyboard, made quick work of his belt buckle and the zipper that tried and failed to keep his cock out of my grasp. It practically sprang out at me, eager to be stroked and caressed. He groaned deep in his throat as his cock throbbed in my hand.

I stroked it up and down, letting my thumb brush across the sensitive head each time. My fingers dampened with the trickle of his fluids. I smiled, victorious.

He reached for my breasts, but I didn't let him touch me. Not yet. This was my night, my way, my time.

"No," I said in that husky voice I'd perfected.

I eased the straps of my dress off my shoulders until it dropped down below my breasts. I unsnapped the front hook of my bra, letting my breasts burst free. One moment they were caressed by the cool breeze that blew down the tunnel, then by the warmth of his mouth, which covered and hungrily sucked one and then the other. I fed them to him, offered up my fruits, but I knew they would not be enough to quench his appetite. I knew what he needed, what would satisfy him. I wanted it, too.

He pushed me against the wall, now, the hand job no longer enough. His need growing, his dick like a shaft of iron in my fingers. His lips gathered the tender flesh of my neck, his teeth sucking it, leaving his lover's mark. Branded for all to know. The thought thrilled me, knowing that I could move through the street, through my days with his mark on me, a symbol, a reminder, of what we had done.

I lifted the hem of my dress up to my waist and ground my cat against him, giving him a sample of what was to come. His moan echoed down the corridor. I almost laughed, feeling the force of my woman power.

His fingers slid beneath my panties, tickled the pink, wet bud until my legs began to tremble. I ripped open his shirt, the buttons popping and dancing along the gray concrete of the subway station. His nipples were mine as I pull them between my teeth, gently biting and nibbling, feeling them harden against my tongue. His dick jerked and throbbed in my hand, seeking a place to relieve itself. His fingers pushed up into my wetness, first one then two. In and out, in and out. My head grew light, as my cat opened and closed around his thick fingers.

I could barely stand, and he knew it. The ground rumbled beneath our feet. The train was coming, time was running out.

He pushed my panties down, and I quickly stepped out of them, our mouths locked in a feverish kiss, tongues slow dragging in contrast to the rapid bump and grind of our hips. He cupped my butt, squeezing and kneading the firm skin, then lifted me, my legs on either side of him, locked around his waist.

The head of his dick pressed against my slick opening. One quick thrust, and he was inside me, spreading me open. My cry bounced off the walls. I squeezed my breasts, twisted the nipples to heighten my pleasure.

He pumped inside me, totally in control, moving faster, deeper, as if seeking some secret place. And he found it.

The train was almost in the station.

I was all sensation. Shudders ran through my body, and I felt that pulse beat deep in my womb, spreading like fire. I was almost there. I could feel it. His dick seemed to grow harder and longer, with his thrust reaching the depths of my sex. I knew it wouldn't be much longer. Neither of us could hold out, even though the vibrations were so exquisite we wanted them to last forever.

And then the tip of his dick touched it, that secret spot in my pussy, and the fire exploded. My body grew rigid, my mouth opened, and my scream slammed against the walls, wrapped around us as the heat of his fluids erupted inside me as his cock jerked and pumped out every drop, setting off yet another climax in me.

For a moment all we could do was hold each other. Keep each other from collapsing onto the gray concrete. His mouth covered mine in a final kiss, as the headlights of the train illuminated the dimness of the station.

His dick slipped out of me and back into the confines of his pants. I adjusted my clothing, picked up my panties and wiped away the evidence of what we had done. He smiled, took my cum-covered panties from me and slipped them into the pocket of his trench coat.

The train roared to a stop in the station and a herd of people spilled onto the platform. We merged with the mix of bodies, ascended the stairs to the street and blended in with the night.

As I lay in bed tingling over my escapade in the train station, I realized that my Margaret self was slipping away. I couldn't wait until she was banished forever. But when the full force of Jade emerged, how would her lust be contained? Could it be?

I planned to ask Anthony during our next session.

Chapter Nine

ednesday finally arrived. I couldn't wait for my day to end so that I could see Anthony, see his expression when I told him what I'd done. I wanted to hear what he had to say, I wanted to see his hunger for me erupt, I wanted to feel him aroused by the visions I would create.

It took all my willpower to keep my Jade self under control. My eyes constantly drifted to the crotches of each and every man who stood in front of me on the train ride to work, who passed by my desk at the office. I wondered what their dicks looked like—long, fat, thin, short, soft, hard. I imagined what they would feel like inside me. I tried to imagine how they did it with their women. Did they have any fantasies? And most of all, did they ever make their fantasies come true?

I had to make at least a half dozen trips to the ladies' room to wipe away my juices, which continued to wet my panties from my erotic thoughts. I'd have to remember to keep a couple of extra pair in my purse. My tits tingled all day. While in the ladies' room hidden behind the stall door, I would take them out of the confines of my blouse and bra and give them a good squeeze, massage them until I could feel my pussy contract. With my free hand I stroked my clit. I couldn't seem to get enough.

I leaned against the stall door, propped my leg up on the seat to give myself greater access to my hungry pussy. I rubbed, tweaked, slid my fingers back and forth across the swollen bud that was as hard as a little dick. I felt it tremble and twitch. My fingers moved faster. Other women were in the rest room, laughing, chatting about their day, their weekends. I stifled my moans as the climax built inside me, humping faster and faster against my fingers. I was almost there. I wanted to hold on to the moment just a while longer, but I couldn't. I shoved two fingers up inside me and instantly felt my walls clamp around them, squeezing and releasing. The orgasm was so intense, so powerful my legs gave out, and I nearly slipped to the floor.

I heard a knock on my stall door. "Are you all right?" some woman asked.

"Yes. I'm fine." I worked to catch my breath. "Thanks," I added. I waited until the room was quiet before I eased out. I caught a glimpse of myself in the mirror. My face was flushed, glowing almost. And my eyes had a distinct shimmer to them. My nipples were still hard, protruding through the soft fabric of my blouse as if the temperature had suddenly dropped. I washed my hands, gave my tits once last squeeze and returned to my desk.

That little interlude would have to hold me until later.

Five o'clock finally arrived, and I couldn't seem to get out of the office fast enough. I wanted to see Anthony. I needed to see him. I wanted to inhale that man smell of him, brush against his cock, see it rise and harden. Yes, I couldn't wait.

By the time I'd reached the front door of Anthony's office, I needed another change of panties. I'd gotten myself so worked up on my way over that I could barely contain myself. Since that evening in the elevator at the mall, my sexuality had been fully awakened, and like a hungry beast, it needed to be constantly fed. My first taste of a real man's cock, and I couldn't get enough.

Anthony was seated in the inner office. As always the lights were turned low, as if he was waiting for a date instead of a client. Amber was nowhere in sight. I closed the door behind me.

Anthony swiveled around in his seat. "It's good to see you." He stood and approached me. For an instant he frowned, his nostrils flaring. His palm gripped the back of my head and pulled me closer. His other hand clutched my pussy and squeezed. I groaned.

"You've been with someone," he said from between clenched teeth. "Tell me," he demanded. His fingers pushed aside my panties, and he slid his thick middle one inside me. "Don't leave anything out. I want to know what you've done," he added, pushing his finger in and out of my cat.

I closed my eyes, letting the waves of sensation roll through me as I began to tell him about my trip to the mall. I didn't leave out anything, and my verbal resurrection of the event excites us even more.

"How did it feel when he first put his dick inside of you?" Anthony asked, his voice so thick I could barely understand him. He slid a second finger up my cat. My legs wobbled and I grabbed Anthony around the neck for support.

"It felt incredible. Like nothing I've ever felt before," I whispered. "And..." He shoved his fingers a little deeper, in and out a little faster. I could hardly breathe.

"Did you like it when he licked it?" He unzipped his pants. My pussy squeezed around his fingers.

"Yes," I stuttered.

"Did you like it on your hands and knees, Jade?"

"Yessss," I hissed, as my climax built inside me.

Anthony pulled one of my hands from behind his head and pressed it against his cock. It jerked beneath my touch.

I squeezed. He moaned raggedly and pumped against my hand.

"Tell me more, Jade. Tell me all of it."

The temperature of the room rose to a dizzying heat, the sound of our hearts racing, our rapid breathing filled the room in a kind of erotic musical.

I could barely think. But I wanted him to know everything. I wanted him to know who he had unleashed with his game of words, his taunts, his hints of what could be. So I told him of the night in the subway. I told him how I took that thick shaft deep inside me right on the platform of the train station. I told him how the possibility of detection excited me, made the act that much more dangerous.

His dick twitched violently in my hand. I stroked it up and down, faster and faster.

No more words.

Anthony suckled my neck, then the rise just above my breasts. His thumb brushed over my clit again and again, and I came over and over, calling his name until the last of his jism spurted across my hand and down my legs.

After we cleaned up, I felt Margaret reassert herself, and I sat demurely on the couch, legs crossed at the ankle. Anthony watched me intently from his perch behind his desk.

"You've come a long way," he said. "You've made a lot of progress. Your inhibitions and your doubts about your sexuality are evaporating day by day."

"Are you this successful with all of your patients?"

He smiled. "You are my prize."

My heart skipped a beat. "Really?"

"Yes. There's been no one like you. But my work, our work isn't complete. I want you totally free. I want Margaret to be the other self, and Jade to be who you are."

"I feel her strength."

"And she'll become stronger. So strong that you'll have to learn how to control her, know when to use her."

I started to tingle again.

"And then everything will be the way that it should. Open yourself to all of the possibilities."

I thought about his last comment as I drifted off to sleep that night. And I wondered what was to come.

Chapter Ten

I

t is the unexpected, the sudden jolt of surprise, that feeds the bright flame of desire. That's the thing that enraptures Jade, the impromptu explosion of coupling, the spontaneous kiss, the abrupt yet knowing caress.

Shortly after the train episode, I was driving along Interstate 91, admiring the sprawling invasion of malls and tract houses along what was once a picturesque stretch of virgin forest and wilderness. The car sputtered once, then twice. I checked the gas meter and noticed my fuel was low, almost empty. In my rush to leave town, I'd forgotten to fill up the tank, and now the threat of running out of gas along the highway was becoming very real.

There was very little traffic, and it was growing dark. Ordinarily, dusk was one of my favorite times of the day but not when I was faced with carrying a gas can and walking on a deserted road in the dark, looking for a gas station. I drove on, not gunning the motor, but keeping a steady pace in quest of a place to fuel up. Finally on the horizon, I spotted one, an old rustic station that appeared to have been there since the Model T car cluttered the roads.

I pulled into the station, breathing a sigh of relief. The attendant, a young freckled teenager, walked out of the building toward the car. He asked me how he could serve me. With the mind of Jade, I immediately visualized taking him back into the building, pushing him onto

his desk where he kept the cash register, unzipping his pants and taking his thick juvenile dick into my mouth until his eyes rolled up into
his head from desire. Then he, overwhelmed by his sudden surge of
pubescent hormones, would clumsily paw my breasts and rub his
huge hairless hands over my crotch before hoisting my dress. There
would be no kissing, no sweet words, just quick animal sex. Teenage
lust gone amok. He'd grab my butt in both hands, thrusting hard and
fast into me, as his pent-up need finally sent him spurting hot seed all
down my leg. I'd stroke his sweating forehead while he tried to regain
his breath, apologizing for cumming so fast. He was still inexperi-
enced, probably a virgin, and screwed like a boy. But when your cat
is hungry, there is no such thing as bad sex, fast sex or amateur sex.
Sometimes a wee taste, a sample can tide you over until you can get
a full helping. I smiled to assure him that I'd enjoyed it and then...

"Ma'am, you want me to fill her up," the teenager asked, breaking
me out of my lusty daydream. "Want me to check the engine, brakes
or tires?"

"No, just some gas," I replied. "That'll be fine. Fill her up."

Yes, fill her up. I smiled at the thought of that. On the other side
of the pump, there was someone pumping gas into his car, a late-
model Jaguar. I couldn't see his face but the silhouette of his frame
looked dangerously familiar.

"Hello," the man said. "How far are you going?"

"Just out for a drive. It's a nice day for it." I was impressed by the
cut of his suit, Italian, maybe Armani. And he had the perfect body to
complement what he was wearing, everything so manly. Rough and
handsome. I instantly felt his power, the pure masculinity of it, and
couldn't think of anything clever to say. Besides, I'd rather hear him
say something, to see his luscious lips move.

He extended his broad hand. I knew he felt something, too,
because although he was now talking to the kid, the heat of his eyes
and body were focused toward me. I could imagine myself on the

floor of the storage room of the station, naked, legs spread wide, about to accept his firm cock into my velvet.

"Are you all right?" he asked when he saw me suddenly lean against my car. My legs were trembling and weak just from the idea of him inside me. His full length, to the hilt.

I struggled to speak. "Yes, I felt a little dizzy, that's all. It'll pass."

He stepped over to me, holding me up by one of my arms as I pretended to be faint. "You need to lie down somewhere. Hey, kid, is there somewhere with a cot where she can lie down for a minute? She's not well."

The attendant, looking younger by the minute, walked up. "What's up? Is she ok?"

Using a low-toned, all-male authoritative voice, the man told the boy that I needed to lie down for a minute before I passed out. He asked the attendant to take a look at how ashen my face was. Inside, I wondered if I really looked that ill or if this guy was so good at this game. Skeptical, the boy insisted he was not allowed to let anyone go back into the private employees' quarters. The boss's orders.

"If it was your mother or someone you really cared about, and she was sick like this, wouldn't you want somebody to show her some kindness?" the man asked. "At a time like this, you have to say to hell with the rules."

That got the kid right where he lived, set him back on his heels. I could see him thinking, *What if it were my mom or my sweetheart?* He was wavering, not sure of the rule of no admittance.

I watched the man walk to the boy, put his arm around him and continue talking softly. The boy, nodding occasionally, matched him step for step as they moved toward the entrance to the old, battered building. Every now and then, a car whizzed past on the highway, going off toward the distance, its bright beams illuminating the road before it. The man smiled and reached into his pants pocket and pulled out his wallet, then he turned where I couldn't see what happened next.

Leaning over, I held my head toward the ground as if I were sick to my stomach. The man helped me straighten up and together we struggled toward the building. Eagerly, the boy trotted ahead of us, but stopped when he heard the automatic click of the pump signaling that the tank was full. He ran to my car and removed the hose from the tank. In no time, he was at the door, holding it open for us and walking us back to the room for employees in the rear.

"You can lay her there for the time being," he said, pointing at one of two cots in the room, happy that he could help. "But you can't stay long. My boss could come at any time. He does that a lot now that his wife left him. He just pops up, surprise visits."

"Ok, kid, now do you have anything to drink, brandy or anything?" the man asked, assisting me onto the cot, lifting my legs. "Then you better get back out front to your business. We won't be long."

The boy got a bottle of whiskey from a drawer in a table across from us, its top covered with frayed girlie magazines and used paper cups. Above the table, there was an entire gallery of naked women in various provocative poses, all either displaying their breasts, butts or sex to full advantage. These boys loved their women, I thought, trying not to smile. The room was small, clean, two folding chairs, a hot plate and a tiny bathroom off to one side, partially concealed by a long curtain.

Once the boy was gone, the man leaned in to kiss me before offering a paper cup of whiskey. "Here, drink this."

I downed the burning liquid like I'd seen actors do in the movies, but I was not prepared for the heat in my stomach. "That stuff is potent. Whew!" It went right to my head.

Then time switched gears. He said nothing else, opened my blouse, and started undoing my bra. I pulled him down into a kiss that continued until my cat began whispering lewd things to my brain. I wanted to say something to him but he covered my mouth with one hand. He smiled like he knew what all men know about women in lust and then he put my hand on his hard, iron cock. It purred in my hand and throbbed like the excited heart of a small bird. I was very wet, maybe too wet. With his other hand, he slid up my dress slowly and stroked my sex while I played with his hair and licked his ear.

Suddenly he got up and began to peel my skirt down toward my ankles, all the while giving me the sexiest look ever. I asked him to let me take off my blouse, and he did, watching me with those eyes. Before I could remove my blouse from my shoulders, he was before me, kneeling with one breast in each hand, licking and squeezing each one, one at a time with the intention of driving me crazy. He sucked them gently, then hard, then gently, flicked at the nipples with the tip of his broad tongue. I squirmed, rolling my hips from side to side involuntarily, the warmth spreading throughout my upper thighs to the quivering valley between my legs. "God," I cried out and came in my panties even before he entered as he licked and sucked my clit through the silk of my underwear. My juices were all over his ample lips.

He was so skilled, so masterful, so graceful and precise. Not one wasted movement. This was how one separated the men from the boys, slow, strong and effortless. He stripped me of my panties and touched me all over, his fingers light and delicate over every curve and contour. I was his slave, at his whim. I submitted to him while he cupped my face with both hands, worked his way up from the downy base of my neck to a delicious spot behind my ear, and I moaned again. No words, silence.

I helped him remove his clothes and lie back on the cot, one leg outstretched. It is the expectation of what comes next that makes sex and desire so great, so addictive. He crawled over to me on all fours like a randy tomcat and began licking me in slow circles along my toes, up along the inside of my legs and long, deep strokes near my drenched vault. I wanted him so badly, I needed to feel him inside me. He brushed his lips lightly against the folds of my pussy, then softly against my pubic hair, and a tingle of electricity ran along my spine. His tongue flattened, assumed an odd shape and moved in a long, sweeping motion from the bottom of my cat to the top, causing my hands to clutch his head tightly. I was panting, screaming inside and helpless. He buried his face in me, both licking and sucking my swollen clit, and my skin felt as if it was melting from heat. While he was doing this with his mouth, his fingers played with my nipples, stroking, flicking, caressing and pinching them.

As I shuddered and squirmed, sensing another orgasm rise within, he straddled me, moving his large dick up and down the opening but not entering. Driving me absolutely nuts. "Give it to me, damnit." I grabbed it when I could no longer take the teasing and placed him inside me, arching my back to receive its full measure. All of it. He looked me in the eyes and screwed me slowly and intensely, so tight, so large. His thrusts grew more forceful and powerful, his rhythm demanding that I match every dip of his hips and push of his pelvis. We were partners, connected by more than flesh. While I may have other lovers, this would always be something separate, something treasured.

Now the thrusts increased in number and power, and I put my lips near his ear. "Fuck me, fuck me, please." He responded until I saw flashes of stars and brilliant bursts of color, and he flipped me over. On my hands and knees, I arched my butt up to meet his cock as he entered me from behind. He was even deeper inside me, hitting something that caused me to miss every other breath. I felt him at the pit of my belly from inside and told him so.

When I looked over my shoulder at him, he seemed sensually transported, his eyes closed and veins standing out on his forehead. He was pounding into me, his finger in my butt, touching his dick from the other side of the thin tissue, and I heard him groaning. He said he was cumming. My legs were shaking, and I did feel faint, and the force of the double penetration made me lose control, and I thought I was screaming loud enough for the boy to call the police. "Oh God, oh God, I'm cumming, cumming." I felt like I was full of cock, and he rammed me two or three more times before he fell onto the cot beside me, and his entire body trembled as if he was having a deep seizure.

He licked my neck and back, and I giggled. We kissed and I tast-

ed myself on his lips and tongue. When we sat up, the boy was standing there, his thin dick in his hand, pumping away. He was so deep
into his fevered dream that he didn't notice us at first. When he did,
he ran away from the door.

On our way out to the cars, the man tipped the boy again, a fifty-
dollar bill this time. As I was getting into my car, I heard the boy ask
the man: "Want me to get your windows? No charge."

I need to come back here more often, I thought, as I got behind
the wheel of my car and pulled out into the night.

Chapter Eleven

I had been nearly three months since I'd met Anthony and become one of his patients, and began the erotic games of the night. Day by day it became harder and harder for me to maintain my Margaret image. It was almost hard for me to imagine how I could have been such a lackluster woman, afraid of my sexuality, afraid of being a woman, believing that the feelings I had were wrong, sinful. Jade was everything Margaret was not. Jade was strong, needy and lusty. Her drive for the exotic, the extreme, the need to be satisfied colored my every waking moment. Once the sensual beast of my buried desires had been aroused, it took a daily dose of willpower to contain them.

Sometimes the urge would be so strong I would have to touch myself under the cover of my desk, even as other staff members walked by and went about the business of working. I couldn't help it.

Lynn noticed the change in me, too, and mentioned it during lunch one afternoon.

"There is definitely something different about you, Margaret," she said, over a mouthful of Cobb salad. "I can't figure it out. There's like a fire around you all the time."

I smiled. "Really. I don't feel any different," I lied.

She looked at me curiously. "Did you take me up on my suggestion?"

"What was that?"

"That you needed a good screw."

At least I had the decency to blush. "Oh, Lynn." I ducked my head.

"You did, didn't you? With that guy you liked."

I took a sip of my iced tea. "I don't want to talk about it," I replied. Although Lynn and I were acquaintances, I didn't feel close enough to her to reveal my secrets, the games I played at night.

"Well, as long as you're happy," Lynn said. "That's what's important."

And I was happy, happier than I'd ever been.

My weekly Wednesday visits to Anthony continued through that first of summer into the fall. During each visit I would mesmerize him with my tales, leaving out no details. I thrilled to watch his arousal, his desire for me. We grew close during that time sharing stories about our lives, our childhood, what we wanted out of life.

Anthony opened a whole new world to me. He gave me books to read, CDs to listen to. He took me shopping at expensive boutiques so that I could look the part of Jade. He took me to wonderful restaurants where I learned to enjoy all sorts of exotic foods and wines. By the time fall arrived I felt confident that I could go anywhere and handle myself in any situation. Anthony worked his schedule so that he could spend all of his free time with me. I became more than a patient, I became an obsession which was just what I wanted. Funny, how the tables had turned. Now I was in control, and I loved it.

My drive for sexual exploits and gratification continued to intensify. Anthony knew what he'd done, the woman he'd created, and he was both fascinated by me and fearful that I would slip out of his grasp. I enjoyed the control I had over him and the games we played. But I wasn't finished yet. I wanted to be the only thing, the only woman on his mind, in his heart. I wanted him to be full of me. I loved the response I got from him when I gave him the blow-by-blow details of my adventures. But I had to increase the stakes.

One afternoon after work I took a trip to lower Manhattan. I needed something special to wear to a party that Anthony invited me to. I strolled into a boutique that specialized in edible underwear, see-through clothes and truly outrageous outfits. That was one thing I loved about living in New York, nothing was out of bounds. If you could think of it, someone had just what you'd imagined and more.

I'd frequented this boutique on several occasions. It was the same one where I'd first seen Amber. What I liked about it was the privacy factor. It was very rarely crowded and the salesclerks left you alone to browse.

When I entered, there was only one other customer, a man. I began looking at some of the new lingerie that had arrived since my last visit. I could feel him watching me. I didn't make eye contact. I moved in and out of the racks and display mannequins, stroking the silky fabrics, rubbing certain pieces between my fingertips.

I picked up a sheer black camisole and held it up to me. I posed in front of the mirror wondering what I would look like with it on. In the mirror I saw him behind me, watching me with a gleam in his eyes and a warm smile on his lips.

My cat began to tingle with hunger. I looked around. The salesclerk was busy dressing the window. I took the camisole, and a set of edible undies and went into the dressing room at the far end of the trendy store.

Within minutes I was stripped naked. I looked at myself in the three-way mirror. I was no longer afraid of my body and what it looked like naked as I had been that day in the bathroom with my mother. Anthony had cured me of that.

I turned this way and that, studying the contours of my body. I cupped my breasts, enjoying the heavy feel of them in my hands, the firmness of them. After seeing Amber's nakedness that night on the beach, and the way her cat hair was cut and trimmed, I'd decided to do the same thing. Now, what was once a bushy, wiry mound was neatly trimmed in a perfect triangle. If you looked carefully you could see the tip of my clit peek out from between my lips, almost as if it was always on the lookout for a quick feel. I smiled at the thought and gave it an affectionate stroking.

I shouldn't have done that. I knew how sensitive I was. The slightest touch, and I was quivering with wanting. I rubbed my finger back and forth against my clit until I felt my juices begin to flow. Heat rushed through me and I began to feel light-headed. My nipples stood erect.

I caught a glimpse of myself in the mirror, and my excitement intensified. I'd never actually watched myself giving pleasure to my body. As I rubbed and stroked my clit I could see it swell. My lips were damp, and my juices glistened against my thighs. My entire body seemed to glow from the inside as my arousal mounted.

My legs began to tremble. I braced myself against the wall and cocked my right leg up on the cushioned stool. I closed my eyes and went to work. The way I was feeling I knew it would be over in a few minutes and that incredible flush of orgasm would flood through me.

I was squeezing my breasts with my free hand, alternating tweaking my nipples. I liked that a lot. I heard my moans as the tension built in my body but I couldn't help it. I was so close, I was cumming. My fingers moved in and out in that practiced move I'd perfected. I gave my clit a light squeeze between my thumb and forefinger, and I nearly collapsed with pleasure.

"Oh, yess, yess," I groaned, working faster. And then everything changed.

I felt a mouth on my cat, a wet hungry mouth licking and lapping. Strong hands grabbed my butt and squeeze, pulling my pussy closer. It was him.

I opened my eyes and watched the action in the mirror. This was so intense. He pushed his tongue right up inside my cat, and it was over. I grabbed his head, feeling as if I wanted to shove it inside me as the climax snatched hold of me and rocked me like a rag doll. Tears sprang from my eyes.

He didn't stop, but increased the pleasure. And I came again in minutes. I felt weak, disoriented, my mind and body were on fire. At first I don't realize that he was pulling me on top of him until I felt the hard knot of the head of his dick pushing against my opening.

He maneuvered my hips until I completely straddled him and he slid right up inside me. It felt so good I wanted to holler. So I just sat on it for a minute, let my body adjust to the thickness. But my body had a mind of its own and began to grind against him, slow at first until we found each other's rhythm.

I braced my hands on his chest to give me more leverage and then I went to work, taking all of him inside me with every stroke. I felt as if he was in my belly, up in my chest, and I still couldn't get enough.

Both of us were breathing hard, and he was groaning like he was in pain—the good kind. Sweat rolled off of us as if we'd come in from the rain. I felt every inch of him. He was so hard I was sure he would snap in half. I reared back so that he could finger my clit. And he knew just what to do. I bit my lip to keep from screaming.

Glancing up, I caught sight of us in the mirror and my pussy instinctively contracted. He squeezed my butt in response and thrust up inside me good and hard. I rode him like a cowgirl trying to tame a wild bronco, with my tits bouncing like two beach balls. I feel incredible, powerful and in total command.

I felt his dick begin to swell inside me, and his groans were out of control. He was going to cum any minute, and I wanted it to be a climax he wouldn't ever forget. I reached behind me and palmed his balls, squeezing ever so gently even as I was pumping.

His mouth opened and all the veins in his face contracted. His entire body grew rigid as he jerked upward one last time, giving me the best that he had. His explosion set mine off, and I collapsed in a heap against him.

We lay there together like that locked in place. I could still feel his dick twitching inside me. He was still hard. And if it weren't for the sound of voices outside of the dressing room, we would have done it again.

Reluctantly, I eased off him, and his cock was still pointing toward heaven. I smiled to myself as I put on my clothes, knowing that heaven was just where he'd been.

More than a bit dazed but totally satisfied I left the store, all thoughts of buying an outfit forgotten.

As I made my way down the street, the slick feel of our juices still clinging to me, I thought about seeing Anthony, telling him every detail in the confines of his office while I watched his cock grow thick with desire.

The party that Anthony invited me to was one of those upscale affairs where everyone spoke in cultured whispers and ate their food on tiny crackers. The women wore gowns and jewels as if they were going to the Oscars, and every man wore some variation of a tuxedo. Music from a live band was playing something you really couldn't dance to, so no one did. They milled around, like in the movies.

"You look beautiful tonight," Anthony said as he offered me a glass of wine.

"Thank you."

I'd finally gotten around to buying myself an outfit, and I have to admit I looked just as classy as any woman in there. My gown was silver, cut deep in the front, almost to my navel. It glittered every time I moved and fit like a second skin. The center split came to within inches of my pussy. Luckily I'd given myself a trim before coming out, or someone would have certainly seen my cat hairs since I'd opted to go pantiless.

"Do you usually take your patients out to these fancy affairs?" I asked, taking a sip of my wine, wishing I could taste Anthony instead. He looked good enough to eat.

He laughed. "No," he said simply. "Does that answer your question?" He looked deep into my eyes, touched my soul. My heart knocked once, then twice in my chest.

"Are you saying I'm special, Anthony?" I probed, turning at the perfect angle to give him a good look at the valley between my breasts.

"Do you feel special?"

"Always a question with a question," I tossed back. "If I had all the answers I wouldn't need you!"

He brushed his thumb across my bottom lip, and I fought down a tremor. "All the answers you'll ever need in life are inside you."

We stood facing each other, so close that the erect tips of my nipples toyed with his chest. I felt his cock jerk against me. I wanted him, right then and there with hundreds of people watching and wishing like hell it was them.

I let my hand casually rub across his crotch while we stared at each other, the heat between us enough to set the place ablaze.

Anthony leaned down and whispered in my ear, "Look around you. If you had one wish tonight, one fantasy you could make come true, what would it be? Don't say anything now. We can talk about it afterward."

He put his arm around my waist and guided me to the other side of the room. That's when I spotted Amber. I should have known that Amber would be at an affair like this. We hadn't seen each other in a while. According to Anthony he'd done all he could for her and was pleased with her success, and she'd moved on with her life.

I must admit, I'd been jealous of Amber. I was certain that she and Anthony were doing it every chance they got. She was incredible to look at. At least while she was Amber and not Amanda. She had a slinky feline quality about her. Very sensual. I couldn't see how Anthony could resist her. It was Amber who actually set me straight about their relationship.

I was on my way up to his office, eager to arouse him with my escapade in the gas station, when Amber got off the elevator. She greeted me with a warm smile. I struggled to do the same. I just knew they'd been up there having at each other.

I started to get on the elevator when she stopped me with a hand on my arm. "Can we talk for a minute?" she asked.

"About what?"

"Me, you and Anthony."

Well, you're damned right I wanted to hear what she had to say. "I have a few minutes," I said as casually as I could.

"Great." She linked her arm through mine like we were the best of friends and guided me back outside.

There was a little diner on the corner. We went in and grabbed a booth in the back. We ordered two sodas.

"I'll try to make this quick," Amber began. "I love Anthony."

I almost choked on my ginger ale.

"I love him as a mentor and a friend. He's done wonderful things for me. He's helped me to be the very best that I can be, not afraid of who I am. I was a mess when I first started my sessions. Now, I'm free, totally free and happy with myself and my sexuality. I owe him everything."

I swallowed, feeling completely silly for the way I'd been treating her, reading things that weren't there. "I'm sorry for being such a bitch to you."

She reached across the table and covered my hand with hers. It felt like cotton. "You didn't know. You had no way of knowing. If I were in your place I would feel the same way. There's nothing for you to apologize for."

What could I say? I'd been an idiot.

"Besides." She leaned back in her seat. "Anthony may be one hunk of a man, but I prefer women. And it was Anthony who helped me to realize and accept that."

Now I was really speechless.

"Don't look so shocked." She laughed lightly. "I'm comfortable with it. Friends?"

I smiled, totally relieved. "Friends."

She stood. "You better get to your appointment."

I scooted out of my seat, and she kissed my cheek, just before she whispered in my ear, "If you're ever interested, I could show you a really good time."

"I don't think so, but thanks for the offer."

We both laughed and walked out.

As I watched her work her way around the room, the epitome of femininity, I wondered who she'd staked out for the night. I was sure they were in for a treat.

I looked at Anthony and watched him watching her. A smile drifted across his mouth. "Let's go out on the balcony," he said.

But before we made it outside, we were waylaid by one of Anthony's doctor friends. Anthony excused himself, and I wandered off alone. I decided to explore the sprawling mansion.

I first went up the spiral staircase to the rooms above. I can't even count how many. They were all beautiful, decorated in gorgeous colors and expensive furnishings. The next flight up was another set of rooms and a stairway that led to the roof.

I looked around. I seemed to be alone and there was no sign that said "keep out." I went up.

What I found was an indoor garden bursting with an array of tropical flowers. The roof was encased in glass, and I could see the entire city. The lights twinkled below. I felt as if I'd been transported to the Garden of Eden, the beginning of time.

I imagined myself as Eve, the first woman who walked the earth, and how she was tempted by the devil to eat the forbidden fruit. And so began man's journey to redemption. I bet Adam and Eve had a ball in that garden, running around half nude, without a care in the world. I stared out the window and all that lay before me. At the moment, I felt as if I had the world at my feet.

Like Amber I'd come a long way as well: overcoming years of doubt, guilt and inhibitions. I still had my moments, my twinges of doubt when I played the games. But in the end I was happy.

I thought about what Anthony said to me downstairs about my fantasy. If I could wish for anything, what would it be? And that's when I felt another presence in the atrium.

I turned away from the window and stared into the semidarkness,

the only light was that of the stars. In the far corner I could just barely make out a shadow.

"Who's there?" I stepped closer. I should have been afraid but I
wasn't. If anything, danger, the unknown was a turnon.

As I drew closer I could see it was a man, seated in the corner.
He stood.

"I hoped you'd come," he said. "I've been waiting all night."

"How did you know you could find me here?"

"No questions." He walked up to me and kissed me, slow and
gentle the way I liked to be kissed. "This is what we both want, why
we're both here."

He brushed my hair away from my face and looked at me so tenderly and with such wanting, it brought tears to my eyes. He kissed
me again, the way lovers do. I felt his arm snake around my waist,
pulling me close. My body was pressed flush against his. I felt his
desire grow and mine met his in return.

Right there, under the moon and starlight we stripped down to
nothing, the way Adam and Eve once were in the garden.

This coupling was different from all the others I'd experienced. It
wasn't a frenzied act, an act of pure sexual gratification. It was something more. And as he moved within me, my legs wrapped tightly
around his waist, my heart opened for the very first time.

Tenderly he sucked my breasts and my hips writhed in pleasure.
My fingers traced the contours of his back as my lips searched once
again for his, the sweetness of them.

The way we held each other, moved together, his dick massaging
my pussy, I truly experienced perfection.

Our hands and mouths were everywhere at once, trying it
seemed to discover all of the secret places.

He took me on my back, on my hands and knees, from the side,
standing, sitting, my legs up, down, spread east and west.

Somehow we found ourselves in front of the window, with the

entire city sprawling beyond us. He lifted me onto the wide sill, his cock still deep within me. He moved in and out, so slow, it seemed as if he was not moving at all. It drove me crazy, and I wanted to buck against him, get him all the way back inside me.

I raised my knees farther up his spine and braced my back against the window. I wanted it, I wanted it now, release, and he knew it. He smiled, dipped his head and pulled a nipple into his mouth. His teeth nibbled it and I felt my pussy contract. He did it again, a bit harder this time. A tremor ran through me.

He took my legs from around his back and stretched them wide, holding them up way above my head. His dick was at the perfect angle. He moved those hips of his in a crazy, circular motion that nearly made me black out with pleasure. Then in and out, real slow and smooth, then faster when he could no longer resist the push and pull of my whip appeal.

He reared back, his head tossed in ecstasy as that first wave hit him like a Mack truck. I thrush another one at him and he shook from head to toe. He looked down at me, his eyes dark, intense and stunned at the same time. He didn't think it would be like that either.

Lowering his head, his tongue dips deep in my mouth as he lifts my ass in both of those big hands and brings it on home.

My cum started at my toes, spiraled up my legs, my thighs, teased my pussy for a hot minute, before scurrying up to my tits, filling them until they felt like they would explode, then rushed to my belly and spread like wildfire to my cat erupting again and again until the full force of his juice finally putsout the flame.

Somehow we found ourselves in a satiated heap on the floor, right there among the beautiful plants and flowers, the sweet scent of nature all around us with the heavens as our blanket. Our own Garden of Eden. I might not have been sure what my fantasy was when Anthony asked me, but now I knew. I'd found it.

Back downstairs among the partygoers there was a new vibe

between me and Anthony, a connection that had not been there before. We both knew it, felt it. Everything had changed in the past hour. There was no turning back.

Chapter Twelve

Back where we began

The cab is easing onto my block now. I live in a great old restored brownstone in Morningside Heights. My little jaunt at the nightclub and my sexcapade on the ride home still has me tingling all over. Looking back over my life, how it all began, the person I once was, makes me realize that everything has its purpose. I was destined to meet Anthony and have him help me uncover the woman I'd become, and at the same time allowing him to be the man I needed.

Yes, some may think its decadent, dangerous, even foolish to have sex in the oddest places. Most women would never do the things I have, but secretly they wish they could. They wish they could live the things that only exist in their minds, in their fantasies. But good loving shouldn't be confined to the bedroom, on cool white sheets. Sex should be a constant adventure, a challenge that opens new doors, expands the relationship, keeps it fresh.

Anthony taught me that. He taught me to let go that time in the elevator, in the employees' lounge at the gas station, in the dressing room at the boutique, on the rooftop under the stars, tonight on the dance floor and all the glorious times in between. He was the first man for me, and I know he will be the last.

I could never figure out how Anthony would always know where I would be, what I would need, what would turn me on. But he did and still does. He's always full of surprises. I've asked him many times—during our early sessions at his office, when we lay in each other's arms at night and relive the pleasures that we've given each other, the erotic games we've played—how he always knows. But he only laughs that deep, sweet laugh of his and tells me that's his one secret. I suppose I'll let him keep it. Not knowing is half the fun.

His car is parked outside when the cab pulls to a stop. I shake my head in amazement wondering how he'd gotten home before me.

Gingerly I walk up the flight of stairs to the front door, my pussy still pulsing from Anthony and my session on the dance floor of the club.

The apartment is dark. I smile and head to the shower, dropping my cum-filled panties right outside the bathroom door. I want him to be sure that I'm home.

Quickly the room fills with steam, the scent of vanilla envelops me. I use my favorite bar of soap and lather my well-trimmed cat, then up to massage my breasts that are still tender from their earlier suckling.

The door opens, and Anthony steps through the steam, joining me beneath the pulse of the spray. He stands behind me, wraps his arms around my waist and kisses the back of my neck.

"I love you, baby. You know that, don't you."

"Yes, I know."

"Did you enjoy tonight?"

"Every bit of it," I respond as his hands begin to travel down the valley of my stomach.

"I was thinking maybe we could go horseback riding this weekend."

I giggle. "Sounds like fun."

"I know it will be," he says, his voice getting heavy and husky.

I feel his cock growing hard against my butt.

"So tell me about tonight," he whispers, pushing me forward.

I brace my hands against the wet tile walls as Anthony slides between my wetness—ready for him, always ready.

"We made love...on the dance floor," I mutter, as he begins to pump inside me. "People...were everywhere...but they didn't know. Ahhh."

"That's what made it...so good, so exciting," he said, sounding a bit breathless as he works faster.

Our wet flesh snaps and pops together. The pace intensifies.

He reaches around and fingers my clit. "Did you like it, baby?"

"Yes. I always like it with you. Always."

And as we came together for the countless time that night, I couldn't wait for our horseback riding escapade. I couldn't begin to imagine what Anthony would have in store. But whatever it was I knew it would be fantastic!

"So tell me again, baby," he whispers. "Did you like what I did to you that night in the elevator?"

I giggle as we slide down the tiles, the rushing water pouring over us like Niagara Falls. I hug my husband tight, kiss him just like that first time, and I look into those beautiful brown eyes. "What part would you like me to tell you first...."